The First Breeze of Summer

A Drama in Two Acts

by Leslie Lee

A SAMUEL FRENCH ACTING EDITION

SAMUEL FRENCH

FOUNDED 1830

New York Hollywood London Toronto

SAMUELFRENCH.COM

THE FIRST BREEZE OF SUMMER was first presented at the St. Marks Playhouse in New York City on March 2, 1975. It was subsequently transferred to the Palace Theatre in New York City and opened there on June 10, 1975. The play was presented by The Negro Ensemble Company, Inc. with the following cast:

GREMMAR .... *Frances Foster*

NATE EDWARDS .... *Charles Brown*

LOU EDWARDS .... *Reyno*

AUNT EDNA .... *Barbara Montgomery*

MILTON EDWARDS .... *Moses Gunn*

HATTIE .... *Ethel Ayler*

LUCRETIA .... *Janet League*

SAM GREENE .... *Carl Crudup*

BRITON WOODWARD .... *Anthony McKay*

REVEREND MOSELY .... *Lou Leabengula Myers*

HOPE .... *Petronia*

JOE DRAKE .... *Peter DeMaio*

GLORIA TOWNES .... *Bebe Drake Hooks*

HARPER EDWARDS .... *Douglas Turner Ward*

Understudies: *Roland Sanchez, Martha Short-Goldsen, Bill Cobbs, Peter Jacob and Samm-Art Williams*

Directed by—*Douglas Turner Ward*

Production Stage Manager—*Horacena J. Taylor*

Assistant Stage Manager—*Jerry Cleveland*

Scenery by—*Edward Burbridge*

Lighting by—*Thomas Skelton* (at the Palace Theatre)
Sandra L. Ross (at the St. Marks Playhouse)

Costumes by—*Mary Mease Warren*

4

TIME: Contemporary

PLACE: A Small City in the Northeast

ACT ONE

Thursday Afternoon through Friday Night in June

ACT TWO

The following Saturday Afternoon through
Sunday Night

DESCRIPTION OF CHARACTERS
(*In Order of Appearance*)

GREMMAR: Milton and Edna's mother, her seventies

NATE EDWARDS: Black male, in his early to middle twenties

LOU EDWARDS: Nate's brother, seventeen or eighteen

AUNT EDNA: Black female, her mid-fifties

MILTON EDWARDS: Edna's brother, father of Lou and Nate, middle fifties

HATTIE: Milton's wife, her early to middle fifties.

LUCRETIA: The young Gremmar, her late teens

SAM GREEN: Black male, his middle to late twenties

BRITON WOODWARD: White male, his late teens or very early twenties

REVEREND MOSELY: Black male, his early sixties

HOPE: Nate's girlfriend, black, her early twenties

JOE DRAKE: White male, his mid-forties

GLORIA TOWNES: Black female, in her late thirties

HARPER EDWARDS: Black male, mid-thirties

6

The First Breeze of Summer

ACT ONE

*It is mid-June, Thursday afternoon, the Edwards'
home. A porch, Stage Left, comprises only a small
area of the Stage. It has a cement floor. A bench
in the Center of the porch, constitutes the porch
furniture. A door at the Right of the porch leads
into the living room, a modest area larger than
the porch, with a writing desk, Up Stage Right;
a dining table with chairs, Stage Center; an armchair, Down Stage Right; and, an armchair, Up
Stage Left. Up Stage Right is an upright piano;
Up Center, a low bench, and Up Left, a small side
table. A flight of stairs, Up Right, leads to* GREM-
MAR'S *room which is also the room where the
flashbacks takes place. The room contains a bed,
Stage Right; a chair, Stage Center; and a dresser,
Down Left.*

At rise, GREMMAR *is standing at the bed removing
a pair of house slippers from a suitcase, which is
on the bed. She is singing a hymn as she moves
around the room. She puts on the slippers and
closes suitcase and puts it under the bed. As she
does, she has an attack of dizziness and falls on
bed. She rises finally and crosses to dresser to
get a fan, discovering a photograph and a string
of pearls. She fondles the picture affectionately.*

GREMMAR. Sam Green, Sam Green. (*She stands the
photograph on the dresser and looks at the string of
pearls longingly.*) Sam, Sam, I've never had something
like this in my whole life—pearls, real pearls.

7

(She puts the pearls on, picks up fan, which she had placed on the dresser top, and starts out of the room. As she does lights rise in the living room and porch areas. Simultaneously, we hear the sounds of Lou *and* Nate *playing a game of sidewalk tennis, off Stage right. As* Gremmar *reaches bottom of stairs* Lou *and* Nate *enter from Down Stage Right.)*

Lou. *(Following* Nate.*)* Where are you going?

Nate. *(At Stage Center.)* Man, later for that—it's too hot!

Lou. Come on, Nate, we're not finished the game yet!

Nate. It's too hot, Lou!

Lou. Nate, its only 18-15. The game goes up to twenty-one!—

Nate. I know what the game goes up to!

Lou. Come on, Nate, it's not that hot!—

Nate. *(Lying on the couch, pulling at his clothing and fanning.)* The hell it isn't!

Lou. Three more points!—

Nate. You beat me, man—you won—all right?

Lou. One more serve then—one more.

Nate. Later, Nigger. Shoot!—no way. That's why the old man and me quit early today, because of this heat, and I am playing that stupid game like some fool! I beat you twice already—what else do you want?

Lou. Just because I'm leading—

Nate. *(Crossing to porch and sitting, Stage Right end of bench.)* So you beat me, all right?

Lou. *(Moving slowly toward the porch and sitting on Stage Left floor.)* Tomorrow don't say the game wasn't over because the score was only 18-15 either!

Nate. Man, I am smothering! . . . Shit! . . . No air— Nothing! Haven't had a decent breeze all summer, if we've had any! Stuff's enough to make you want to slap Jesus on Easter Sunday! *(*Lou *laughs*

despite being miffed.) Can't eat . . . sleep . . . can't
half breathe . . . itching all the time. Take a bath
and you're still itching . . . Can't even get worked
up over my woman Hope. You know I'm in trouble.
(*Laughing despite his discomfort.*) You know what I
oughta do? I ought to form me a march . . . get me
some folks together and march on this crap! Demon-
strate! Sit down in the street! "Down with heat! Heat
ain't too cool! . . . Ban the good old summer time!"
—a march! . . . Even in the winter time, when somebody mentions the word "summer," I begin to sweat.
I hate the word, man!

(GREMMAR, *inside the living room, is seated on the
piano-stool, commencing to play a hymn. Lou
crosses to doorway. He pauses for a moment,
listening. Finally, he crosses Stage Left of porch.*)

Lou. Gremmar's been good to us, you know that,
Nate? (NATE *nods.*) I mean, when you think of older
people—right? She's so easy to talk to—I mean you
can—sit down and talk to her about . . . anything
just about, you know? . . . Anything . . . more than
Mom and Pop. (*Pause.*) You know what I mean, Nate?
    NATE. Yeah . . . yeah.
    Lou. (*Sits Stage Left end of bench.*) Nate, do you
remember that scooter Gremmar brought you a long
time ago?
    NATE. (*Shifting to his back, fanning.*) Yeah, I re-
member . . .
    Lou. (*Pause, smiling, reminiscent.*) She brought me
that cowboy outfit, too—remember? (NATE *nods.*) Two
guns and a holster . . . and silver bullets! (Lou *rises.*)
and that ten-gallon hat!
    NATE. (*Hot, shifting again.*) Yeah, Mr. Bad Nigger
—the Lone Ranger himself! Damn hat falling down
all over his eyes . . . running and bumping into shit

and wondering why . . . Couldn't half see . . . Running to Mom and crying about hurting yourself.

LOU. (*Laughing.*) Yeah, I'd have worn them to bed at night if Mom hadn't ripped them off me. (*Pause.*)

NATE. Man, this humidity's a regular bitch! (*They are interrupted by the appearance of* AUNT EDNA, *moving up to them laboriously from off Stage Left.*)

LOU. Hi, Aunt Edna.

EDNA. Lord Jesus, I'm telling you! The Lord is punishing somebody today, child! I just wish he wouldn't include me in on the whipping though. I didn't do nothing! Just minding my own business! (*She kisses* NATE *and* LOU *on the cheek. They assist her as she sits and begins to wipe her face with her handkerchief.*) I'm telling you boys, it's hot out here today! Just let me catch my breath a minute! (*Hearing* GREMMAR *playing the piano.*) I see Mama's home from work for the week-end a day early! . . . Lord, it feels good to get them feet! Things was killing me! Dogs was hurting! Yes sir! . . . (*With feigned indignation.*) Louis looks so cool! How come you look so cool, Louis?

NATE. You know them colored people, Aunt Edna—just love the heat!

LOU. (*Slightly embarrassed.*) I can feel it! . . . I mean . . . it's hot, but—

NATE. Listen at Lou, Aunt Edna—doesn't want to be accused of being a nigger for the life of him!

LOU. I just said—

EDNA. We-ll, I guess I must not be one, because I can't stand it—never could! No sir! Yes, Lord, this must be Egypt—can't be the United States!

NATE. Got your flowered dress on today, huh, Aunt Edna?—all fixed up, trying to turn some heads today! I know—I know what you're trying to do!

EDNA. I'm glad you do, son, because I'm a wilted flower today! My leaves done dried out today!

NATE. Oh no!

EDNA. Gets a little cooler now, then you're talking about something else!

NATE. You don't have to tell me!—

EDNA. Might be snow on the roof, son, but there's plenty of fire inside! (*All laugh.*)

NATE. All right, all right now!

EDNA. *Plenty* of fire inside!

NATE. Oh I know that! I can see that! I been watching you! "Look at Old Aunt Edna fluttering and flapping her eyes at Old Mayberry."

EDNA. Lord, children, don't put that old man on me, now! I don't deserve that now, do I? I don't want no old man. I want a *young* man! Yes, a young man!

NATE. I don't know, Aunt Edna, maybe you'd better stick with Mr. Mayberry. One of these young cats might be too much for you!

EDNA. Well too much is better than too little, and Henry Mayberry is to little! (*They all laugh uproariously. During the laughter, the black out drop is flown in and the three walls—for the flashbacks—SAM, BRITON and HARPER are sneaked in behind it.*) Well I got my breath here now. (*Having difficulty rising.*) Give me a hand, son. These dogs of mine ain't coöperating!

NATE. (*He moves to help her.*) I'm going to take another damn shower.

(*They begin towards door. LOU lingers outside before exiting Down Stage Right across the apron. GREMMAR, is playing and singing "Leaning On The Everlasting Arms." NATE and EDNA enter the living room; EDNA gives her shopping bag to NATE to hide it from GREMMAR. NATE, heads upstairs and exits Stage Right. EDNA starts singing and GREMMAR looks around and sees her. They hug and EDNA crosses to Down Right arm chair and sits. HATTIE enters from kitchen, which is up Left. She*

*is carrying a tray with four glasses of iced tea.
She gives one to* EDNA *and one to* GREMMAR *and
stands Stage Left of piano—joining the singing.*
MILTON *enters from kitchen area, carrying a
garden spade and gloves. He crosses to table and
sits in Stage Left chair, also joining the singing.*)

GREMMAR. (*Finishing.*) I just love that hymn!—
such a beautiful song!

HATTIE. (*Crosses to desk and puts tray on it.*) Yes
it was. (MILTON *and* EDNA *agree.*)

EDNA. Sounded like Mrs. Armstrong down at the
church, Momma.

GREMMAR. (*Laughing.*) Oh child, I'm just sitting
here banging—just banging, that's all. I could play like
that child, I'd be doing something.

HATTIE. (*Crossing Down Stage between* EDNA *and*
GREMMAR.) Yes, for somebody' that's so disagreeable,
she's certainly a good organist—and just loves Milton!

MILTON. Oh now, Hattie!

EDNA. A little sweet on Milton, huh, Hattie?

HATTIE. Yes, Jesus! The first thing Sunday morning,
here she comes. "Hello, Hattie," and then just gab,
gab, gab to Milton!—

MILTON. Hattie—

HATTIE. The two of 'em just chin to chin! Tickles
me!

EDNA. (*Winking at* HATTIE, *who laughs.*) Better
keep your eye on him, Hattie—keep your eye on him!
I know Lucille—

MILTON. Hattie, you shouldn't be telling stories like
that!—

HATTIE. (*Crosses to table, gives a glass to* MILTON,
and sits in Stage Right chair.) I'm just teasing you,
Milton.

GREMMAR. Yes, yes she is, son, just teasing.

MILTON. Well I wish she wouldn't. I'm in the Lord's

house . . . wouldn't be right to be . . . nasty to the woman . . .

GREMMAR. No that's right . . . that's right . . .

HATTIE. Milton can tease but can't stand nobody to tease him.

EDNA. (*Laughing.*) Just chin to chin, huh, Hattie? Lucille is something else! Yes, Lord! (*They are silent a moment as* LOU *crosses apron from Stage Right to sit on porch bench.*)

HATTIE. Well did Tom show up today?

MILTON. Half drunk as usual . . . I'd just as soon do without the man . . . Been advertising for somebody for two weeks now, and we haven't had one call —not one! (MILTON *rises, and crosses to* GREMMAR *Stage Right between arm chair and piano.*) Can't get young people interested in plastering today . . . Don't want to do a day's work—want something for nothing —fast cars and loud radios! . . . Haven't had one call! (LOU *rises, enters and stands at the door.*) Louis comes this summer, that'll be somebody at least. Lord knows we need the help. (LOU *frowns, sighing heavily.* HATTIE *looks at him.*)

HATTIE. (*Starts toward kitchen with two empty glasses from the table, sees* LOUIS, *and stops.*) Louis, what are you frowning about? You aren't coming down with something, are you?

EDNA. This kinda weather—

LOU. (*Sighing heavily again.*) I was . . . thinking about . . . about working some place else this summer.

(*There is a moment of strained silence, and glances are exchanged by the others.* HATTIE *puts the glasses on the small side table up Left.*)

MILTON. Somewhere else?— Where else?

LOU. (*Shrugging, peeved.*) I don't know . . . just . . . somewhere . . . else, that's all . . .

MILTON. Lord knows, Louis, I certainly was depending on you. Nathan and I could use all the help we can get, for all Tom is worth.

LOU. For goodness sakes, do I have to plaster every summer?

HATTIE. (*Steps to* LOUIS.) You don't have to do anything but die, Louis.

MILTON. Is there something wrong with the way I make my living?

LOU. I didn't say that!—

HATTIE. (*As* EDNA *concurs.*) He certainly didn't, Milton, now don't start exaggerating—

GREMMAR. No he didn't now . . . he didn't . . .

LOU. It's . . . it's—all I said was—

MILTON. All the work we have—people calling me up and me promising, and here I am trying to plan ahead—can't get nobody to work for me and—

EDNA. Milton, if the child don't want to—

MILTON. It's not a question of wanting to—

LOU. Pop—

MILTON. His brother didn't want to drop outta school to help me, but he did. Louis is only in high school. It's not like I was asking him to sacrifice his education—

LOU. Well I'm not Nate—

GREMMAR. Louis, son—

MILTON. What's the matter, don't I treat you right?

LOU. Pop, I'd rather do something else—

MILTON. (*Steps toward* LOUIS.) I can't help what you want to do. You're working with Nate and me this summer! (*Cutting him off as he starts to speak.*) I'm still the father of this house!

LOU. How can anybody forget it!

MILTON. Now that's enough back talk from you, young man!—that's enough! Here—here I am sweating to put food on the table—providing—we need the help—you wanting me to help you with your college tuition next year and—

Lou. (*Crosses Down Stage Center to dining table.*) All right, I'll pay for it then!—

Gremmar. (*Trying to lighten the atmosphere.*) Come on, you all. Let's not fight. Let's be happy— let's be happy now. (*She begins playing softly.*)

Lou. Gremmar, I will pay for it!

Milton. (*Crossing Down Stage Center to Louis.*) I don't care what you do next summer—that's your business! This summer you're working for me, and I don't want to hear another word about it! (Milton *starts toward kitchen.*) Louis just wants to be the black sheep of the family—

Lou. (*Starting for the porch.*) Oh for goodness sakes! Just because— (Lou *storms out,* Milton, Edna *and* Hattie *exit kitchen arguing about* Lou.)

Gremmar. Louis! Son?—Sam! Sam!

(Gremmar *crosses to Stage Center. She stops suddenly, faint, and sits in the Stage Center chair at table— holding the pearls. The lights dim in living room to special on* Gremmar, *and black out drop is flown out to reveal Wall No. 1* [Sam]. *As lights rise in bedroom,* Lucretia *enters from Stage Left —stands at dresser holding a hand mirror.* Sam *enters from Up Stage Right and crosses to stand at foot of bed.*)

Lucretia. Oh, Sam, these are lovely!—they really are! They're so pretty!

Sam. You like 'em, huh, babe?

Lucretia. Oh, Sam, you know I do—I really do! (*Looking almost in awe at herself.*) They're so pretty!— What are these—pearls, Sam? Is that—

Sam. (*Proudly, cockily.*) They're pearls . . .

Lucretia. Oh . . . (*Continuing to look at herself and then giggling nervously.*) I— I've never had something like these before, Sam—real pearls . . . Makes me feel like a . . . a . . . rich lady or something . . . (*She laughs, glancing at him for his approval, and then looks again in the mirror, gently fingering the pearls.*) They're so beautiful . . . tiny . . . sparkling-like . . . Pearls! (*She stops, a look of horror on her face.*) Sam, how much did these things cost you?

SAM. (*Laughing.*) Come on, babe, you're not supposed to be asking me no questions like that! What's the matter, don't you have no manners? Your momma didn't bring you up no better than that? Don't worry about it!

LUCRETIA. (*Laughing.*) Lord, Momma's eyes'll pop wide open when she sees this. She think's everything's supposed to be so simple. Nothing flashy. These certainly would be flashy to her. Probably just jealous, I guess, Poppa not being able to give her nothing like this . . . (*Pause, stepping to* SAM.) They didn't cost a lot, did they, Sam? Just tell me that. You don't have to tell me nothing more—all right? They weren't, were they?

SAM. (*Shrugging, nonchalant.*) Oh . . . not too . . .

LUCRETIA. (*Watching him.*) That's the truth?

SAM. Baby, you asked me, and I just told you—

LUCRETIA. All right, all right— (*Looking down at pearls again.*) Sam . . . I— I'm going to have to hide these things—

SAM. Hide 'em? . . . Huh? . . . Baby, what are you talking—

LUCRETIA. Sam, I know— I know they'll make me give 'em back to you. I know they will!—

SAM. Give 'em back? How come you're going to have to give 'em back? It's my money. I do with it what I want. Nobody—

LUCRETIA. Sam, it's not that! . . . That's not it . . . not it at all . . . Sam, I'm only seventeen . . . They —they might think I shouldn't be . . . be having things like this—so expensive looking. I mean, you know the way things are around here—work so slow—

you know what I mean? I mean, they're kinda funny that way . . . So afraid somebody's going to be showing off with something new—

SAM. For Pete's sake, babe! I—I didn't buy them things for you to have to hide—

LUCRETIA. I—I'll wear 'em only around you, Sam. (*She hugs him.*) When we're together—all right? Momma and them don't ever have to know. Sam, it's either that or I'm going to—to have to give 'em back to you. (*She crosses to dresser and looks in hand mirror.*) I mean . . . pearls, Sam! Who around here has some pearls?

SAM. (*Sighing heavily, helplessly.*) Lu, baby . . . Look, sugar . . .

LUCRETIA. What's the matter?

SAM. Well . . . (*Pausing, shrugging, and then blurting out.*) Look, sugar, they—they ain't—ain't no real pearls! (*He sighs, looking at her and then dropping his eyes, expecting the worst.*) They . . . ain't . . .

LUCRETIA. (*Surprised.*) Oh . . . they're not?

SAM. (*Sighing heavily.*) They're not real . . . They're . . . imitation—that's what the woman said —imitation . . .

LUCRETIA. You mean they're . . . fakes or something?

SAM. (*Quickly.*) No, they're not fakes . . . I mean, you know, they're supposed to be pearls, but they're not, you know? . . . I mean, they look like 'em, but they're not. You know what I mean, babe? I mean, they're supposed to look like pearls, but they're something else— (*Stopping, exasperated.*) Oh, I don't know, baby, they're just—just . . . imitation, whatever the hell that is! How should I know! (*Pause.*) I—I just . . . I just don't want you to think you got some thing you don't, that's all . . . And there's no sense anybody else thinking it too . . . I certainly don't want you hiding them . . . (*Sighing heavily.*)

LUCRETIA. (*Turning to the mirror again.*) They sure

do look real if they aren't . . . They cost a couple of dollars then?

SAM. (*Turns and steps Stage Right.*) Yeah . . yeah . . . a couple, you know . . .

LUCRETIA. Well, Sam, that's better then, isn't it? I mean, if Momma and Poppa think they're fakes— I mean, imitation—then they won't mind then, will they?

SAM. I don't know. You know your people better than I do . . .

LUCRETIA. Oh Sam, thank you!— Thank you, Sam! (*Rushing to, embracing, and kissing him.*) I'll wear 'em—okay?

SAM. (*Somewhat bewildered.*) Damn, Lady, you sure did put me through the mill over them things—

LUCRETIA. (*Pulling away.*) Sam, where's your uniform? I thought there was something funny about you! Sam, how come you're not at work? It's not time yet for—

SAM. (*Turning Down Stage.*) They—they give me the afternoon off—

LUCRETIA. The afternoon? How come?

SAM. (*Hesitant, shrugging.*) I—I don't know, baby . . . Man come up and told me . . . Some . . . some kinda slow up on the tracks somewhere—accident— trains wasn't coming in . . . tied up . . . Didn't need all the porters in the station . . . Said to take the afternoon off. So I took it. (*Laughing nervously.*) Didn't have to tell me twice . . .

LUCRETIA. (*Not really comprehending.*) You get paid for it, don't you?

SAM. (*Boldly.*) Oh yeah . . . oh yeah . . . Something like this . . . wasn't our fault . . . they pay us . . .

LUCRETIA. (*Watching him.*) Oh . . .   (LUCRETIA *starts to dresser as* SAM *sits dejectedly on foot of bed. She crosses to him.*) Sam . . . are you all right? What

—what are you telling me? I know—I know you're trying to tell me something—

SAM. (*Rising.*) Yeah . . . yeah, I'm trying to tell you something! . . . Yeah! . . . I'm trying to tell you I ain't been to work in two days, babe—two days! . . . Yeah, I got the afternoon off. Yeah, I get the rest of my life off as far as those people are concerned down there— (*He crosses Left Center.*)

LUCRETIA. (*Sighing heavily and then looking away.*) Oh Sam! . . . Sam, what happened? Sam, you haven't been to work in—in . . . *two* days, and you're just telling me?—

SAM. There wasn't no need, baby—

LUCRETIA. What do you mean no need? Don't you think—

SAM. I thought I could get another one! . . . I thought I could . . .

LUCRETIA. Sam, what happened? (*With great consternation.*)

SAM. (*Slowly.*) Babe, do you remember me telling you about Pop?

LUCRETIA. You mean that old man at the station—the porter?

SAM. The man's a doctor, Lu! (*She looks at him, amazed.*) He's a doctor, baby! So help me! You should hear him rattle off that stuff! I mean, the man knows it backward and forward—he is! He doesn't have no reason to lie to me, babe! Look, I see his—whatever they call the damn thing—his degree—all in Latin and junk! He carries it with him—no lie!—in his back pocket! He showed me!

LUCRETIA. A doctor? Lord Jesus!

SAM. You never heard nothing like that in your whole life, have you? A porter!

LUCRETIA. What—what in the world is he doing down there at the station, Sam?

SAM. (*Crossing Stage Right to foot of bed.*) He told me one day—quiet-like . . . We was sitting there eating lunch. He likes me, you see. I don't know why. We just kinda took a shine to one another—right away. I don't know . . . Maybe because I didn't ask him to explain hisself, you know? I mean, I didn't try to take nothing away from him, that's what he told me . . . (*Pause.*) He couldn't get no work, babe—

LUCRETIA. Sam, there's plenty of need for doctors around here—

SAM. He couldn't make it baby. You have to eat. What are you going to eat—promises? Damn right we get sick. But who the hell can pay for it? He couldn't make it. The man had to eat! A hell of a lot of sick people, but no cash babe! (LUCRETIA *sits on bed as* SAM *crosses Stage Center.*) Colored people weren't ready for colored doctors, or maybe colored doctors weren't ready for colored people. I forget the way he put it, but something like that . . . He said he didn't mind helping folks, but he didn't realize how much it was necessary for him not to be hungry—to not be worrying about next month all the time . . . (*Pauses.*) Wanted it simple, he said . . . just plain simple, you know, babe . . . Didn't want to have to think . . . or feel . . . or even care . . . the hell with it . . . Gave it up . . . He's a porter, so help me God, a porter, down at the station. (*Pause.*) He was . . . you know . . . doing his job . . . He's pushing this cracker's bags . . . Cracker's got enough bags for everybody in this whole town piled up on top of Pop's cart. He's pushing the damn thing, and it's heavy, but he's pushing, smiling and whistling, happylike . . . And I don't know, for some reason one of the bags comes tumbling down and falls on the floor. The thing is, it splits— A couple of things break. The cracker claims they're from— I don't know whether he's lying or not—from Paris or Europe, one of them damn places. And all of a sudden, he's getting red in the face. He's yelling and making a big stew, calling Doc names! Calling him boy this and nigger that, and Pop—Pop is just . . . just standing there—like he's supposed to take it, smil-

ing and apologizing. (*Pause.*) He's got his mind—
Pop—on what he is now, not what he was. He ain't
no goddamn porter, but he don't want nobody to
change it. He's got it all figured out! So that stupid,
dumb, doctor-porter is taking all the cracker's crap!
Taking it, talking to himself, reciting that stuff from
his medical books! . . . Well, I couldn't take it! So
I hightail it over to where they standing, and—and
before I could catch myself, I'm telling this cracker
off! I got my hand, my fist, my nose into his, and I'm
screaming at him—yelling at him—calling him the
names he's calling Pop. And that stupid Pop—Doc—
is pulling at me—yanking at me, because he knows,
because he's made it all so simple! And he's struggling
with me! And I'm yelling at the cracker: "This man's
a doctor, goddammit! You oughta be carrying his bags,
you sonofabitch! Don't you talk to Dr. Savage that
way! And Pop is crying almost, because I promised
I wouldn't say nothing to nobody! That's what's getting him! He's begging me and half-crying for me to
shut up! And then all of a sudden, he pulls out that
damn piece of paper and tears it into shreds—just rips
it up! (*Pauses.*) Well . . . to make a long story short
. . . that's it. I mean, that's it . . . I wasn't worth a
good minute after that . . . Right on the spot . . . on
the damn spot! (*Pauses*) I turn around . . . on my
way out . . . and there's . . . *Pop* . . . doing penance
for me . . . cleaning up that bastard's shit . . . smiling, apologizing . . . kissing ass! . . . If he's mad,
he's mad at me and not at the cracker—for messing
up his goddamn, stupid world . . . (*Laughing suddenly and sitting in chair Stage Center.*) Baby, I'm so
miserable, it's funny . . . miserable . . .

LUCRETIA. (*Taking the beads off and crossing to
SAM.*) You—you take these things right back where
you got it from! I—I'm not going to take your last
penny! (*She gives the pearls to him.*) I don't care if
they are fakes! (*Crosses to Stage Right.*)

SAM. (*Going to her with the pearls.*) They're yours,

now put 'em on! I bought 'em for you! I wanted you
to have 'em! I wasn't thinking about no money! I just
wanted you to have 'em—because you'd look nice in
'em! . . . Now come on! (*He places them around her
neck.*) That's it . . . that's it, baby, . . . Yeah, now
you're looking good . . . just like—like a—a plate of
fried tomatoes and gravy, huh? . . . Huh? (*He forces
a laugh. She crosses back to dresser. He turns away.*)
Yeah, yeah, he's got it all figured out . . . figured
out . . . To him it's so simple . . . The rest of us
make it so complicated . . . (*Turning to* LUCRETIA.)
Lu . . . baby . . . I'm going to have to . . . to . . .
pull out for a while. (*She groans softly, turning away.*)
There's . . . there's nothing here, babe—nothing. Two
days I been looking and hating, babe . . . But the
word's out—everywhere . . . down in the fields too.
They got me, babe . . . (*She is silent, choking back
tears.*) Just for a while . . . won't be long . . .

LUCRETIA. (*Takes a step to him.*) Will you—will
you take me with you?

SAM. Come on now, babe . . . come on! It ain't no
kinda life for you, not the way—

LUCRETIA. (*Crossing to* SAM.) Sam, I want to go
with you!—

SAM. No! No! . . . No! . . . You may as well stop
—stop talking! It's no life, now take my word for it!
. . . Running here . . . Running there . . . riding
that damn boxcar . . . (*Sighing, shaking his head.*)
It'll only be a little while . . .

LUCRETIA. Oh Sam . . . Sam— (*She crosses Up
Stage between bed and chair.*)

SAM. (*Crosses to* LUCRETIA.) Just a while . . . What
am I supposed to do, babe—stay here and . . . and
. . . starve! There's nothing here! Pop's seen to that!
(*Sighing.*) You think I want to go? I'll just be a . . .
while, baby. You know I'm not going to stay away.
(*Again trying to laugh.*)

LUCRETIA. That's probab.y what you told the last
one where you've been.

SAM. (*Turning away and crossing Down Stage.*) Come on, will you, babe—

LUCRETIA. You probably got a whole string of 'em waiting for you to come home to—probably. You . . . black . . . nigger! (*He turns and slaps her face. She turns away, holding her face.*)

SAM. (*Sighing heavily.*) Oh goddammit! (*Pause.* LUCRETIA *crosses to dresser.*) Look, sugar, I'm sorry . . . I'm sorry . . . Don't call me stuff like that, huh? . . . Not stuff like that . . . It ain't that simple for me, babe—not like Pop . . . like Pop.

LUCRETIA. (*Crosses to* SAM.) Sam? . . . Sam, I—I want to talk to you about . . . something— (*She starts to speak, but he kisses her. They embrace, passions rising, and fall on the bed.*)

(*BLACKOUT. In BLACKOUT* NATE *can be heard singing Off Stage. The lights rise in living room and porch, where* LOU *sits brooding.* GREMMAR *rises and crosses to stairs—meeting* NATE *as he moves down the steps to the porch. He pinches her cheek lightly.* GREMMAR *exits up stairs and Off Stage Right, carrying her glass and fan.*)

LOU. (*Tersely, upon* NATE'S *arriving.*) You've given it all up for daddy haven't you. Nate?

NATE. (*Stopping.*) Given what up?

LOU. School. I thought you wanted to teach so much. That's what you said you wanted to do before.

NATE. I know what I said—I know it. The man needs help, Lou. So what am I supposed to do, huh? Yeah, I wanted to be one. (*Crosses Stage Left of porch.*) So what the hell, everybody can't be one. Besides, they have enough people doing it without me.

LOU. (*Shaking his head disconsolately.*) Gremmar told me about . . . about your dropping out of—quitting school because of me.

NATE. (*Shrugging, sitting.*) Yeah, well, I figured as

long as one of us went, what the hell's the difference. You were smarter than me . . . in the long run . . . had the best chance of making it, so . . . (*Pause, wiping perspiration from his forehead.*) I suppose I was pissed-off at first. You know the way the old man can make you feel guilty—like if you don't help him you're going to be cast into the fiery furnace . . . you know . . . So, who knows, maybe I didn't have any other choice. What the hell, it's a . . . trade . . . It's honest . . . making my own living . . . not cheating anybody. I don't know, I might go back some day.

Lou. You've been saying that for three years now, Nate.

Nate. And I might be saying it for five more! I *might* go back—I might! I . . . I think about it . . . Anyway, it's not that important anymore . . . not like it used to be . . . You get out of school, and you see some things different . . . Those people don't make that much bread anyway. Oh who knows! I'm plastering—it's all right it is . . . I'm outside a lot . . . Nobody but the old man standing over me, and . . . I can handle him . . . I'm better than he is anyway. He knows it. He may not admit it, but damned if he doesn't know it! . . . He knows it . . . So I'm no teacher . . . I'm a plasterer.

Lou. (*Softly, intensely.*) I . . . I could've gotten a job in the hospital this summer—in the lab maybe . . . an orderly or something . . . Instead I—I have to do what?—plaster! I could be picking up some experience maybe—something that has to do with what I want to do in . . . college. But no . . . I have to fool around working for him—

Nate. That's between you and him, Lou. I—

Lou. (*Rises, crosses Down Stage edge of porch.*) Don't remind me! (*Softly, agitated.*) Riding in the back of that . . . truck . . . like some . . . dope!

Nate. (*Crossing Down Stage to level with* Lou.) So ride in the front—all right? I'll ride in the damn back! I don't give a shit if people think I'm a dope! Let 'em think what they please!

Lou. Oh, it's—it's not just . . . that! (*Sighing heavily.*) Plaster . . . you get sores all over your hands . . . stuff all in your eyes! . . . Damp . . . dirty! . . . It's—

NATE. Man, you can wear some gloves—and we have a pair of goggles, if that's what's bothering you. I use to wear 'em when I first started. (Lou *sits on edge of porch Down Stage.*) It's not too bad, Lou . . . Shit, I have a business . . . I'm saving a little bread . . . Don't have the damn bill collectors on my tail . . . I have enough threads and all that . . . It's no big deal . . . not worth all that. Shit, you are what you are, you know? (*There is a sudden, loud, crashing noise— the sound of breaking glass. NATE and Lou both jerk around, startled, toward the noise.*) What the hell— (*The noise also startles MILTON who is just entering from kitchen area.*)

MILTON. (*Crossing Stage Center of living room.*) What in the world?—

(NATE *moves quickly off the porch, around the side of the house, exiting Down Stage Right from apron.*)

NATE. Come on, man! (Lou *follows, as* HATTIE *rushes into the living room from Upstage Right, followed by* GREMMAR.)

HATTIE. Milton, a rock! A rock! Just come flying through the window, breaking glass all over the place!

MILTON. A rock?

GREMMAR. Lord have mercy!

HATTIE. A big piece of rock!

MILTON. Those two boys! Louis! Nate! (NATE, *again followed by* Lou, *moves back onto the porch and into the living room, meeting* MILTON.)

NATE. Pop, it was Tom!

Lou. We just saw him running down the street!

MILTON. Tom? What in the world is Tom throwing stuff through my window for?—

GREMMAR. Trash, nothing but trash, that's all. It's a shame!

NATE. I don't know. He's mad, that's all I guess. I stopped down at the Picket Post for a couple of seconds after work. Tom was there—drunk, as usual. Already drunk up his pay. And he started bugging me to lend him some money. I told him I wasn't going to give him one red cent. I told him you weren't either, so there was no sense asking. He got teed off, and I guess he still is.

MILTON. That man! I'm going to break his neck!

NATE. He's probably back at the Post.

MILTON. (*Moving toward the kitchen area exit with* NATE *and* Lou *leading.*) Break his neck! Fool man!

HATTIE. Milton!

GREMMAR. Come on back, son.

MILTON. I—I'm just going to talk to the man, Momma. (*He continues out with the boys.*)

HATTIE. Milton, Tom ain't worth you getting in trouble about.

GREMMAR. (*Rising, moving after him, preceded by* HATTIE.) Milton, there's no sense going down there and getting yourself in a lot of trouble over that man. It's not worth it son. Just because he wants to show his ignorance is no reason why you have to. Use your head now, Milton. Use your head.— Don't leave with anger in your heart, son— Don't go—don't go— (*She stands in kitchen area looking helplessly after them. Her thoughts turn inward as she continues to mutter softly, "Don't leave." The lights fade to special on* GREMMAR. *Lights rise in* LUCRETIA'S *room. She enters from Stage Left and stands at dresser in same position as* GREMMAR, *then crosses to bed, as special on* GREMMAR *fades out. She sits on the bed, staring emptily.* SAM *appears at the door, Up Stage Right, a traveling bag in his hand. He stands with uncertainty before stepping into the room and setting down the bag.*)

LUCRETIA. (*Without looking up.*) Are you leaving now, Sam?

SAM. In—in a minute.

LUCRETIA. (*Rises and crosses to dresser.*) I . . . I know . . . I know you'll be gone forever.

SAM. (*Attempting lightness, and steps to* LUCRETIA.) I'll be back . . . just as soon as I get me a job . . . Won't take me long. (*Laughing.*) Soon as I get me a job . . . be right back here! . . . Maybe—maybe in one of them brand new buggies! (*Forcing more laughter.*)

LUCRETIA. (*Despondently, crossing to bed.*) You must be getting touched in the head, Sam. (*She is silent for a moment, and then quickly without looking.*) Sam? (*He stops. She places her hand on her belly and sits on foot of bed.*) Sam, feel here please!

SAM. Do what?

LUCRETIA. Feel here—right here . . . Come on, feel it, Sam!

SAM. (*Frowning, sitting beside her on bed, and putting his hand on her belly.*) What—what is it I'm supposed to be feeling?

LUCRETIA. It's your child there, Sam.

SAM. You . . . you got a . . . a . . . child in there? —a . . . baby? (*She nods.*) How you—how you—you seen a doctor?

LUCRETIA. No, but—

SAM. Then how the hell you know if you haven't—

LUCRETIA. (*Rises, crosses to dresser.*) Sam, I know! . . . I mean . . . I know! . . . I'm a woman, ain't I? I ought to know—

SAM. (*Rises follows her.*) Don't play with me now, Lucretia! I don't like for people to play with me like that—.

LUCRETIA. Sam, I know—I know! . . . I told you! (*He turns away, and crosses Stage Right.*)

SAM. (*Turns to* LUCRETIA.) Shit! . . . Shit! . . .
Baby—baby, I have to go! . . . I—I can't stay here!
I stay here . . . what . . . what's that . . . child
going to live on, huh? I mean, what's he going to feed
on if I don't have no work? . . . Can't have no star-
ving child in there now. You got one, you sure of it?
(*Turning to face her.*) You ain't just . . . just doing
it to me?

LUCRETIA. Sam, why do I want to lie?

SAM. (*Moving to her and sitting with her on the
foot of bed.*) Look, baby, now look . . . look . . .
You—you just get in touch with me, you hear? You
. . . you get on over to that doctor in town, and when
you're sure—real sure—you just get in touch with
me—

LUCRETIA. Sam, don't change on me—people
change—

SAM. I ain't people, dammit! I'm Sam Green . . .
Ain't nobody but Sam Green! Now . . . now you do
what I tell you, Lu, you hear? I'll—I'll let you know
where I am, and you get word to me the first thing—

LUCRETIA. (*Standing, moving away from him, Stage
Left.*) Oh, man, just . . . just . . . just . . . get out
of here before I start bawling please! Please? . . .

SAM. (*Watching her for a moment, and then rises
and crosses Down Stage Right.*) Yeah . . . yeah . . .
Trains don't slow down much for niggers. (*He hes-
itates. She suddenly turns away from the dresser and
rushes to him, embracing him.*) Soon—soon, sugar-
lump, you'll look over at that goddamn old door—

LUCRETIA. (*Whispering.*) Please don't swear, Sam
—not right now . . .

SAM. (*Matching her softness.*) You'll look at that
old door, and you know who'll be standing there? . . .
Yeah, that's right—me! Yeah, me! And you know
what? You know what, baby? I'm going to have me
a brand new buggy outside—all shined up and ready
to take you back—

LUCRETIA. Don't talk simple, Sam. Just—just come back on a mule if you have to.

SAM. I'll be back. You'll see . . . You just keep watching. (*Brings* LUCRETIA *Down Stage Center.*) Every once in a while, you look out that old window . . . look way down the road there—way down there. You'll see me . . . see me coming back. Done struck it rich! Yeah! (*He smiles and then kisses her. She clings to him for a moment and then lets go. At first somber, he straightens and swaggers toward the door.*)

SAM. (*Turning to her.*) See you, sugar, when I'm rich! (*He moves jauntily out the door. He is gone, enveloped by the darkness.*)

LUCRETIA. (*Crosses to doorway Up Stage Right.*) You're touched in the head! . . . You know that, Sam? (*She stares into the darkness.*) And don't you go messing with all them other women neither, man! You're supposed to be working hard and providing for Little Sam—that's what I'm going to call him! (*She crosses back into the room, looks at photograph on dresser, and then sits on the bed and stares emptily.*) Sam, I'm scared . . . all of a sudden I'm scared!

(*LIGHTS fade, and* LUCRETIA *clears Up Stage Right. Laughter is heard. The LIGHTS rise on the porch. It is the afternoon of the next day, and Wall No. 1 is flown out to reveal Wall No. 2* [BRITON] GREMMAR *and* LOU *sit on the porch front, playing scrabble.* GREMMAR *is Stage Right, and* LOU *is Stage Left on bench.*)

LOU. (*Quickly.*) That's a word!

GREMMAR. It is?

LOU. Yep—cilia.

GREMMAR. Cilia? What in the world—you mean "silly," don't you?

LOU. (*Laughing.*) No, Gremmar—"cilia."

GREMMAR. Now, Louis, what kind of word is that? I never—

LOU. (*Straigtening, reciting proudly from memory.*) Okay, let's see. It's the . . . hair-like outgrowths of certain cells, capable of vibrating—no!—vibratory movements, or the . . . small . . . hair-like . . . processes extending from certain plant cells . . . often forming a fringe or hairy surface . . . as on the underside of some leaves . . . that's a term in biology.

GREMMAR. (*Smiling—impressed.*) Yes, I figured it was something from all you were saying about it. That's what it means, huh? Yes, well, that's right, baby, learn all you can about it—learn all you can. Lord, just spouting it out like butter! (*She studies the letters on her rack and then begins to fit them into the maze.*) Is that right? . . . I don't want you to think I'm cheating now.

LOU. (*Teasing.*) Gremmar, I'm really impressed! And another thing—you didn't cheat! Yes, that's right.

GREMMAR. I know it's right . . . Beseech! . . . Beseech! . . . I beseech you therefore, brethren, by the mercies of God, that ye present your bodies . . . a living sacrifice, holy, acceptable unto God, which is your reasonable service . . . And be . . . and be not confirmed to this world: but . . . be ye . . . transformed by the renewing of your mind, that ye may prove—that ye may prove what is good . . . and acceptable . . . and perfect . . . will of God! . . . That's Romans, twelfth chapter—St. Paul talking . . . ! Yes, Saint Paul . . . ! Yes sir! . . . And that's what I've been trying to do all these years, abiding by the will of the Master—doing the right thing—all my life . . . Yes, abiding by the will of the Master . . . Making myself acceptable unto the Lord, Which is my reasonable service! Yes sir!

LOU. (*Pause.*) Gremmar, sometimes, you know, you —you try to do the right thing— I mean, I've been trying to—just like you did—

GREMMAR. (*Reaching, patting his hand.*) I know you have, baby. I see you trying, and the Lord'll bless you—he will.

LOU. I mean, I want to be a doctor or scientist—right? And you have to study hard—right?

GREMMAR. That's right. Oh yes!

LOU. I don't know . . . The colored kids at school . . . most of 'em . . . they fool around. They don't care! And just because I don't act silly as they do—because I know what I want to do—they call me a bookworm and really— I mean, *really* get jealous because I study hard. I mean, they try to make me feel guilty. You know what I mean?

GREMMAR. I know, I know.

LOU. And next year, half of 'em, after graduation, won't be able to get near a college, and then they'll be complaining about having to work in a . . . a . . . gas station! or . . . or . . . doing construction work . . . or being a . . . garbage collector, maybe—things like that . . . Well . . . I just don't want to do things like that . . . I mean, it's . . . it's . . . you know . . . de . . . grading . . . (*Shrugging.*) I mean, it's all right and all, but . . . I want to be . . . better than that. You—you know what I mean, Gremmar?

GREMMAR. I know . . . Oh yes, child, yes, I know. But that's right . . . that's right. You strive, you hear? You just strive on for the highest you can get. There's nothing wrong with that. No, you've got the brains. Lord yes, you can see that playing this here old game with me. Yes, you have the brains. No reason why white folks have to get it all—no reason at all! (GREMMAR *rises and crosses Down Stage.*)

LOU. I know . . .

GREMMAR. Yessir, keep right on striving, you hear? (*Lights fade down to special on* GREMMAR.)

LOU. (*Nodding softly.*) Yes, ma'am.

GREMMAR. That's it, baby . . . that's it.

(*Special fades out, and* GREMMAR *and* LOU *clear Stage Left. The LIGHTS rise on* LUCRETIA'S *room.* LUCRETIA, *an apron on, runs into the room, followed by* BRITON. *He attemps to kiss her.*)

LUCRETIA. (*Resisting.*) Mr. Briton, I—I haven't finished my cleaning, and—and I got cooking to do—
BRITON. You've got plenty of time for that!—
LUCRETIA. Mr. Briton, please! Your father—your father finds out—he's got a mean temper! I—I can't afford to lose my job—my child!—
BRITON. They're gone, and you know it!—you know it! You want to see? I'll show you, and then what kind of excuse will you have? (*He goes to the door up Stage Right.*) Hey you old sonofabitch, are you down there? You're gone, aren't you, you and your old bitch? —to another one of your goddamn parties! Tell this black woman here who won't kiss me that you're gone and won't be back until after she kisses me at least once! Tell her so she won't be scared. Tell her, Daddy! (*He stands, feigning listening, and then laughs, moving back to her.*) You see, they're gone!
LUCRETIA. Sometimes they come back early.
BRITON. (*Crosses Down Stage and into room Stage Center.*) And most of the time they don't. You think they get all fixed up like they do just to come running back to spy on us? (*Attempting to kiss her again, but she resists.*)
LUCRETIA. Mr. Briton, I—
BRITON. You've been . . . been teasing me, that's what you've been doing—teasing this little white boy ever since you came into this house draggin' your knapsack and little kid behind you—
LUCRETIA. Mr. Briton, I haven't . . . I most certainly haven't—
BRITON. The hell you haven't! . . . You know damn well what you've been doing—the way you look at me. Those quick little glances . . . That sneaky little

smile you've got—when you're serving the table—rubbing yourself against me—

LUCRETIA. Mr. Briton you're lying, that's not true!

BRITON. Oh yes it is!

LUCRETIA. Shhhhhh. (*Turning and stepping Stage Right.*) I think—

BRITON. They're gone, goddammit! (*Crossing to chair.*) I could do something, you know? . . . I could . . . I damn sure could . . . I could tell my old man about you . . . I could walk up to him and say "Old Man, I got something to tell you about your servant girl . . . It's about her teasing, Old Man. She isn't no servant girl, she's nothing but a great big tease, that's what . . ."

LUCRETIA. Mr. Briton, I'm nothing of the kind, I never did anything to make you think . . .

BRITON. (*Sensing her fear, teasing her more.*) Yep, I just might tell him—old bird . . . You can never tell about me. I'm adopted, you see, I ain't really one of theirs. They all think I'm half-crazy anyway. Yeah, who knows, I might just walk on down these steps when he comes and tell him—

LUCRETIA. I'll . . . I'll . . . I'll leave . . . I'll take Little Sam, and I'll leave right now!— (*Moving toward the dresser and removing clothing from the dresser.*)

BRITON. (*Stopping her.*) Jesus Christ!—you—you— Oh, Jesus Christ! (*Looking at her in amazement.*) Do—do you *really* think I'd do something like that— You know I wouldn't dare, don't you? (*Pause.*) Don't you? What do you take me for, huh? I'm teasing you—just teasing you, that's all! My daddy—which he really isn't—he's the one that holds threats over folks here in Roanoke. He's the one that does stuff like that! (*Pause.*) You didn't believe I was serious, did you? . . . Did you, Lucretia?

LUCRETIA. (*Softly.*) Yes . . .

BRITON. (*In animated disbelief.*) Oh man! . . . Oh

man, I mean, what the hell do I look like—some . . .
goon or something? Is that what I look like? Jeee-sus
God, are you gullible! . . . I mean . . . I mean, is
that why you wouldn't let me kiss you, is that why?

LUCRETIA. (*Turning away.*) Things would start . . .
Things would start . . . (*Crosses Stage Right.*) Mr.
Briton I have to get back to work—

BRITON. (*Stopping her.*) Why do you call me that?

LUCRETIA. Your daddy said—

BRITON. My daddy, my daddy, hell! Well he's not
my daddy. He's nothing of the kind! He says he is,
but he's not! My father, I don't know where the hell
he is—who the hell he is! My mother either! I don't
give a good damn either, for that matter! . . . My
daddy thought he was impotent. That's why it's
"Briton, you do this; Briton you do that!" I remind
him of his impotence! . . . Every time he looks at me,
that's what he sees—and he hates . . . he hates to
think of it! (*Laughing ruefully.*) They never thought
they were going to have anything. Ten years they did
it—humping each other. They didn't give a good goddamn about each other. Ten years! And nothing, not
even a dribble from his cock! . . . And so, it was me
. . . me! "That one over there!"—me! . . . And then,
through some miracle, Jamie comes along! No more
use for me now! You—you should just see the way
they go on and on about that little bastard! I'm a
mistake . . . "My daddy" hates to think of himself
as possibly having been so much of a weakling for so
long—no, not with all his illusions of grandeur! But
that's what the hell he thought, until they finally
managed to scrape the bottom of the barrel of their
sexual powers and dug up Jamie . . . He looks dug
up too!

LUCRETIA. (*Trying to push him out of the room.*)
Please go, Mr. Briton, and let me get to my work.

BRITON. (*Grabbing her arm, stopping her.*) You're
. . . you're really a pretty woman, Lucretia . . . you
really are. You're not . . . artificial—like those high-

society dames they try to set me up with. (*Pause,
looking tenderly at her.*) We have a lot in common,
you and me, Lucretia! You know that?— Both of us
are outcasts! That's what we are around here. No
wonder it's—

LUCRETIA. I—I have to go . . . I—I have to clean
the upstairs and the downstairs too. And your father
—Mr. Woodward likes a bite to eat when he comes
in— (*He grabs her and kisses her. She starts to
struggle but yields, embracing him—pulling away
after a moment, turning away Down Stage.*)

BRITON. (*Frowning.*) What—what's the matter?
. . . You—you didn't like it? . . . I—don't kiss like
your . . . black friends out on the grounds?

LUCRETIA. Shhh! (*Crossing toward the door.*) It's
them— I told you! I told you! And I haven't got
nothing done!

BRITON. (*Following her.*) This isn't the last time, is
it, Lucretia?

LUCRETIA. (*In near panic.*) I have to go! Mr. Briton
please don't let them catch you in my room!

BRITON. (*At the door, whispering.*) Tomorrow,
Lucretia, do you hear? . . . Lucretia? . . . Tomorrow! We're outcasts—okay?

(*LIGHTS fade to black Off Stage, we hear* REVEREND
MOSELY, HATTIE *and* MILTON *talking. As lights
rise* GREMMAR *is crossing from kitchen area into
living room, where she reaches Stage Center.*
REV. MOSELY *enters from kitchen carrying a cup
of tea followed by* HATTIE, MILTON [*carrying a
bible*], *and* LOU, *also entering from kitchen.*
GREMMAR *sits Down Right armchair;* MILTON *sits
Stage Right at table;* HATTIE *Stage Left of table,
and* LOU *on piano stool.*)

MOSLEY. Therefore, I said, therefore doth my soul
keep them!

GREMMAR. (*Simultaneously with* MILTON *and* HATTIE.) Amen, Reverend. (NATE *and* HOPE *enter from porch—see* REV. MOSELY *and start to leave. They are stopped by* HATTIE *who indicates for them to sit in Up Left armchair.*)

MOSELY. (*A slight reasonance in his voice.*) The mercy of the Lord is everlasting to *everlasting* . . . Just think of it—everlasting, children, upon them that fear him—*fear* him and his righteousness unto children's children! (*Again, "amens" from the three adults.*) For no other—no *other* foundation can any man—*any* man lay than which is in the Saviour! (*"Amens."*) We're here to give testimony . . . to give thanks—to say, "Thank you, Mr. Jesus, for the many blessings you bestowed upon this household this past week. Thank you, Jesus!"

MILTON. That's right, Reverend.

GREMMAR. Thank you, Jesus.

MOSLEY. (*Crossing Down Stage in front of table.*) And he has—oh yes, he has! Yes sir! We must count our blessings tonight, children. Let's count 'em—count 'em—each in his own way, each in his own time. For surely, children, we are pilgrims in this strange and weary land!—

MILTON. All right, Reverend!

GREMMAR. Amen, sir—amen!

HATTIE. Have mercy, Jesus—have mercy! (*Softly.*)

MOSELY. (*Crossing Up Stage Center behind table.*) And HE is our refuge and strength, though the waters, young people, roar and be troubled, the scriptures says: "And the mountains *shake* with the swelling thereof!" (*"Amens" from* HATTIE, MILTON *and* GREMMAR.) All right now, children, each in his own way . . . in his own time . . . let the spirit of God—let his spirit move you—let it move you, and give thanks for his bountiful goodness this past week . . . Perhaps sister Lucretia will play something on the piano now to help us feel the spirit of God moving.

GREMMAR. (*Rising, going to the piano;* LOU *rises*

from piano stool and sits on bench.) Certainly, Reverend, be glad to.

MOSELY. Softly now . . . softly . . . Let Jesus come into your hearts tonight now. Let him in . . . Open up your hearts now . . . Give him the key . . . Let him unlock the door of your heart and steal softly in and move you, children. (*She begins to play "Blessed Assurance," humming softly as she does. The others join in, singing softly.*) Softly . . . softly . . . each in his own way . . . his own time . . . softly . . . (NATE *coughs, shifting nervously, attempting to mask his reluctance to be present. He glances from the corner of his eyes at* HOPE, *who is less nervous.* LOU, *like* HATTIE *and* MILTON, *is pensive and stares down at the floor.*) Let him move you now . . . *move* you. Let the Father, Son, and Holy Ghost walk on into your hearts, my friends, and move you. Don't fight him . . . don't fight him . . . Let him in.

MILTON. (*Reading strongly.*) Yea, though I walk through the valley of the shadow of death, I will fear no evil, for thou art *with* me!—

MOSELY. (*Softly but intently.*) Yes, yes! (*Resuming humming.*)

MILTON. Thy rod and thy staff comfort me! . . . Thou preparest a table before me in the presence of mine enemies; thou anointest my head with oil; my cup . . . *runneth over!* (*Closing the bible.*)

MOSELY. Yes, yes! (*In response,* GREMMAR *sings louder.*)

MILTON. (*Rises and crosses behind Stage Right armchair.*) I want to thank the good Lord for walking with me the past week.

MOSELY. Uh-huh . . . uh-huh . . .

MILTON. As he has done each week in the past. He has been by my side— I know it!—because I know him —I know the Lord—yes I do!

GREMMAR. All right son! All right! (*Singing again.*)

MOSELY. Yes, yes! (*Singing.*)

MILTON. Been by my side! I know him! Many have fallen by the wayside since last we've gathered together, through death or through the wages of sin, but the good Lord has spared this family to see another week!—

MOSELY. All right now, sir—all right!

GREMMAR. Amen, amen!

HATTIE. (*Softly.*) Have mercy, Jesus!

MILTON. And I want to let Jesus into my heart now, and I want to say, "Thank you, Jesus!"

MOSELY. Thank you, Jesus!

GREMMAR. (*Echoing him and then singing louder.*) Thank you, Jesus!

MILTON. And I want to thank you, Lord, for preparing a table . . . preparing a table and providing . . . and providing . . . (*Unable to control his emotions, stopping and crying slightly.*)

MOSELY. Take your time, brother . . . take your time . . . take all the time the spirit gives you—

GRAMMAR. Bless you, son—bless you!

MILTON. (*With difficulty.*) Thank you, Lord, for . . . preparing a table and . . . and providing for me and my family (*Crosses to* GREMMAR *and hugs her.*) and looking after Momma—

GREMMAR. (*Stops playing, but everyone continues to sing.*) That's right, son . . . that's right now . . . "Looking after Momma."—that's right— (*Resuming singing.*)

MILTON. (*Standing Stage Left of* GREMMAR.) And . . . taking care of her needs and all . . . And we . . . we ask your continued blessings, Lord—your continued blessings . . . and ask your help—help us to grow stronger—stronger in your way, Saviour—stronger, so that— (*His voice cascades into soft sobbing,* REV. MOSELY *crosses to* MILTON *and helps him to sit at table Stage Right chair.*)

MOSELY. That's all right, brother, that's all right . . . It's good to let the Lord fill up your heart—it's good! Let him fill up your heart as he filled up your table! Let him fill it up! For I will fill up your heart if you let me, he said! Fill it up! (*Crossing behind Stage Right armchair.*) Each in his own time . . . his own way . . .

HATTIE. (*After a moment, rising quickly.*) I just want to say, "Thank you, Jesus—your continued blessing!" (*Sitting.*)

MOSELY. Amen . . . amen . . . That's right, sister Hattie. Thank you Jesus, and your continued blessings! (*Humming and then stopping.*) Softly . . . softly . . . each in his own time . . . own way . . . (*As the others sing.*) Maybe one of the young people would like to . . . would like to say something—testify.

MILTON. Amen.

MOSELY. Maybe one of the young people would like to say something . . . remember his kindness—his goodness. You don't have to be embarrassed in front of Jesus—no sir!—not in front of the Saviour! No sir, children, because he understands us all . . . understands us all! (NATE *is more uneasy and sinks down in his seat.* MILTON, *attempting not to be too obvious, looks at* NATE, *who shrugs, keeping his head down.* MILTON *glares at him.*) Trust in the Lord, young people! Let him do the talking for you. Give him the key! Can't unlock your hearts unless you give him the key now! Give him the key, young people! (HATTIE *looks at* NATE *and gestures for him to rise.* HOPE *nudges him.*)

GREMMAR. All right! All right! Give him the key! All right, sir!— (NATE *stands finally, reluctant, angry, nervous, trying to conceal his feelings. He begins to mumble his words. The others continue singing.*)

NATE. I'd . . . I'd like to say . . . as a . . . young person . . . I'd like to say . . . thank God for . . . for . . . for . . .

MOSELY. Take your time, son . . . Give him the key now . . . Don't forget the key! He'll move you!

GREMMAR. That's right, Nathan—that's right.

NATE. For all his blessings . . . this week . . . (*Sighing heavily.*) And . . . last week . . . And . . . for safety . . . and . . . good health . . . and . . . for all his . . . continued blessings . . . (*He sits dropping his eyes, embarrassed.*)

MOSELY. (*Crosses Stage Left toward* NATE.) All right, son, all right . . . You don't have to feel no shame in front of Jesus—no shame! He promised us that! He is willing and able to do your talking if you ask him. (*Crosses Stage Center.*)

GREMMAR. (*Suddenly, zealously.*) Yes he will! Yes he will! I know—I know, 'cause I'm a child of the king!— (*She rises, crosses Down Stage Right, in front of armchair.* LOU *watches her, entranced and intrigued.*) A child of the *King!* And I want you to know—I want you to know that I'm walking up the *King's* highway! (*The others sing throughout her testimony, stopping to comment but always resuming singing.*)

MILTON. (*Picking up her enthusiasm.*) That's right, Momma!

MOSELY. Uh-huh, uh-huh!

GREMMAR. And ain't nothing—nothing going to stop me from making heaven my home, because he promised me a room—

MOSELY. All right, sister, let him move you!

MILTON. Go ahead, Momma!

HATTIE. (*Softly.*) Have mercy, Saviour.

GREMMAR. Promised me a room in one of his many mansions!—

MOSELY. (*And* MILTON.) Yes, yes!

GREMMAR. And though the way has been long and weary, I want you to know, Lord Jesus, that I will persevere!

MOSELY. Persevere!

MILTON. Amen, Momma!

GREMMAR. Persevere, because I am sustained in *his* strength that has made me whole! Because he alone—he alone can sustain. He is the King!

MOSELY. Yes!

GREMMAR. The King! And I want to thank my King —thank you, Jesus, for your blessings—for your tenderness. Thank you, Jesus, for being a rock in a weary land full of sin and destruction! Thank you, Jesus, for letting me *lean*. You've let me lean, Jesus, on your mighty arm, and let me lay my tired body against your soft bosom!

MOSELY. Let him talk to you sister!—let him talk!

GREMMAR. I am weak, but you are strong, Lord! And heaven is my eternal home! And I will be there— I will *be* there on Judgement Day, because I have tried to fulfill your ways! I have walked the straight and narrow path, keeping my eyes on the sparrow—on the sparrow!—ignoring the temptations along the way! I'm marching on up the King's highway with nothing but heaven on my mind—my feeble mind. I will be there!—standing in front of your judgement bar to listen—

MOSELY. To listen—

GREMMAR. To listen to your sweet and mighty voice say—

MOSELY. Tell him what it's going to say, sister!

GREMMAR. To hear your sweet and mighty voice say: "Well done, good and faithful servant—well done!" Have mercy, Jesus, and bless your precious name!

(HATTIE *starts singing "Well Done;" the others join in.* LOU *has watched* GREMMAR's *demonstration in awe and reverence. Caught up in the fervor of the moment, he stands suddenly—crosses Down Stage behind* MILTON *mesmerized, trembling, almost oblivious to the others. The others, somewhat shocked, stop singing for a moment and watch him.*)

LOU. I—I want to—to thank God . . . I want to thank God! I do—I really do! (NATE *looks at him in*

disbelief.) I want to thank him . . . thank him! . . .
I want to thank him for sparing my family . . . for
food and strength . . . for school . . . for church . . .
for Gremmar . . . (*Turns to* GREMMAR *and hugs her.*)
For providing a table . . . For helping me to . . .
to keep Satan out of my life . . . and . . . letting me
into his heart . . . and touching me!— (LOU *crosses
Down Stage Right in front of arm chair.* NATE *frowns,
suddenly realizing* LOU's *seriousness. He shifts in his
seat, disturbed. The others resume singing.*) For giving
me the key and . . . and . . . unlocking the door to
my heart to serve him . . . And . . . and nothing's
going to stop me, like Gremmar said—Satan—nothing!
Because I—I want a room in one of your mansions,
Jesus—I really do! And I promise—I promise to serve
you, because I love you, because . . . because I . . .
I love you, Lord . . . I love you and—I give myself
to you, and I'll continue to do what you want me to
do . . . and pray . . . and not sin . . . and obey
your commandments—I really will! Because I . . . I
want to go to college and study medicine and . . .
science . . . and biology . . . and keep my eye on
the sparrow, and pray and . . . and not get tempted
. . . and trust and . . . and . . .

(GREMMAR, HATTIE, MILTON *and* REV. MOSELY *move
to him, comforting him, and take* LOU *off into
kitchen, with* GREMMAR *following.* HOPE *starts to
follow, but* NATE *tugs at her and they exit Stage
left off porch area.* GREMMAR *stops Up Left and
turns Stage Right as lights fade down to special
on her. The lights rise on* LUCRETIA's *room and
special fades out.* GREMMAR *clears Stage Left.*
BRITON *and* LUCRETIA *lie together on the bed, their
clothing awry.*)

BRITON. (*Silent, and then sitting up suddenly and
crossing Stage Center.*) I've decided, goddammit,

Lucretia! Just now, laying here with you! I'm not going back to school! I don't have to! Christ, I'm over twenty-one! I don't have to go back unless I want to! The only reason I went was because he wanted me to. He wanted me to because my brother Jamie, which he's not really, didn't want to be a lawyer like him. That's why I went—to please him. Somebody—somebody in the family had to be a lawyer. Somebody—one of us—just *had* to be a lawyer because he is! Well, to hell with him! He's so proud of Jamie, let Jamie do it for him! . . . What do you think of that lady?

LUCRETIA. If . . . if that's what you want . . .

BRITON. Well that's what I want, lady. I want you! (*He crosses to bed—kisses her.*) That's what I want . . . I don't want to be a crooked lawyer like him. He's a crook—I know he is! He—he carries himself too perfect—too stiff—too proud—too much like a—bigshot! (*He hops out of bed and begins strutting around the room in imitation.*) Like some—some . . . proud-assed turkey! That's how he walks. (*She laughs.*) Doesn't he?

LUCRETIA. (*Laughing.*) Yes!

BRITON. Man, you talk about somebody not knowing how to have any fun, it's that man! (*Sobering suddenly.*) Not unless he's with Jamie . . . then he laughs. (*Strutting again, laughing only slightly.*) Big, powerful, important man like him just couldn't have taken ten years to have a kid. (*He is silent and then sits on the side of the bed next to her, thinking.*) I'm not going back. (*Rising again and pacing.*) No sir . . . I'm going to . . . I'm going to . . . to just . . . I don't know—just get the hell out of here and—and . . . *bum!*—and fly high! I'm going to be like a great big bird, Lucretia, and fly all over this world! (*He spreads his arms like a bird and spins around the room, "flying."*) Fly until I get dizzy—until I see it all, and then—then I'll come flying back to wherever you are! (*He "flies" toward her, leaping on the bed beside her and tickling her.*)

LUCRETIA. (*Laughing, again resisting.*) Briton, stop!

BRITON. (*Nestling close to her.*) You like me, don't you, Lucretia?

LUCRETIA. (*Softly.*) Yes . . .

BRITON. That's good . . . yeah, that's what I need . . . yeah . . . You need it too, you know . . . outcasts like we are . . . (*He lies down with his head on her lap*) You're soft, Lucretia . . . good and soft . . . like a pillow. (*Pretending to snore.*)

LUCRETIA. Briton . . . if . . . if you don't like them people out there in the field . . . how . . how come —how come you like me . . . I'm no different.

BRITON. (*Sitting up.*) The hell you're not! . . . You're . . . goodlooking . . . (*Rises and crosses Down Left Center.*) And besides . . . besides . . . your face isn't always screwed up and pissed-off-looking like theirs—like they want to kill me and not my *daddy!* I'm nice to 'em. I'm polite . . . I'm always talking with them and clowning around when I'm down there —just like I do with you . . . It pisses the old man off! It really does! You should see his face, Lucretia! You've seen his face when he gets pissed off!

LUCRETIA. (*Standing suddenly at foot of bed.*) Shhhhhhh!

BRITON. (*Crosses to LUCRETIA.*) Oh come on now! Every time we're together!— They went out to dinner . . . And . . . she'll get drunk and sloppy sick with her *southern charm,* of course. And so will he. When he's ready, they'll come home bound by their drunkeness and flop into bed. We could stay here the whole night, so stop worrying. (*Sits on bed and pulls LUCRETIA down beside him, and kisses her.*)

BRITON. Your mouth is really sensual, you know, Lucretia? You Negras really have sensual mouths— not like us white people—

LUCRETIA. (*With difficulty.*) Briton . . . when I was gone today—

BRITON. Hey, I was wondering where the hell you were. I was getting lonesome.

LUCRETIA. I . . . I was at . . . I was at the doctor, Briton. (*He frowns.*) He . . . he says I'm . . . going to have another baby—

BRITON. (*Turning sharply to her, stunned.*) He says you're . . . what?

LUCRETIA. That's what he told me, Briton. I—

BRITON. (*Staring hard at her and then rising.*) You —you're not saying it's . . . *mine,* are you? You're not—

LUCRETIA. Briton, it can't be nobody else's. I don't see nobody but you. I don't hardly go out of this house—

BRITON. Who—who the hell did you go to—some colored doctor across town?

LUCRETIA. Yes, but—

BRITON. Well you—you just get yourself to a white doctor! (*Turning away, angry, trembling.*) You just get yourself to a *white* doctor!—

LUCRETIA. Briton, the man did a test or something! He—

BRITON. (*Rises and crosses Stage Left Center.*) But I made sure!—

LUCRETIA. (*Looking toward the door.*) Briton, not so loud!

BRITON. They're gone, goddammit! I keep telling you that! I'm not going to that goddamn door again! (*Pacing.*) I made sure! I took precautions with you— everytime! Unless . . . unless the—the last time—or —sometime you told me it was all right!—

LUCRETIA. I—I thought it was!

BRITON. What do you mean, you thought? Jesus Christ, Lucretia!—

LUCRETIA. I thought . . . I thought it . . . was . . .

BRITON. You're trying to trick me, aren't you? You black—

LUCRETIA. Briton, I'm not—

BRITON. (*Turning angrily away Down Stage Center.*) Trying to trick me!— One of those—those . . . *people* out there knocked you up and now you're trying to blame it on me!—

LUCRETIA. (*Rising, straightening, and crossing to* BRITON.) I ain't one of those flighty girl friends you bring around here, boy!—

BRITON. Wait . . . just wait . . . just let me get my mind together . . . Sometimes I have trouble getting my mind together, you know? (*Pacing.*) I have a little trouble . . . These people around here! . . . Look, Lucretia . . . that—that white doctor . . . (*Sitting on the foot of the bed and easing her Down Stage Right of him.*) Look, we'll get you over to him —or the black one, if that's what you want, and . . . and we'll get a job done on you.

LUCRETIA. Briton, I'm not going to get rid of it, if that's what you mean—

BRITON. Oh come on, Lucretia, you have to—

LUCRETIA. I don't believe in that kinda stuff—

BRITON. Well you better believe in it! . . . You have to do it, Lucretia, because—Lucretia, don't tie me down to thoughts . . . Don't tie me down to something I'm not ready to think about.

LUCRETIA. (*Rises, crosses Down Right.*) Briton, I've thought about it— I'm going away from here—

BRITON. (*Rising.*) Where?—and saddled with two kids? Look—

LUCRETIA. I'm not going to do what you want me to! . . . I'll tell your father I have to quit—I have to go on up North, but . . . I'm not going to do it! . . . I'm not going to tell nobody if that's what you're worried about—I won't.

BRITON. (*Steps to* LUCRETIA.) No . . . no, I know you wouldn't . . . You should, but you wouldn't.

(*Pacing, Stage Center.*) So many things I want to do
. . . so many goddamn places I want to be—sometimes
all at the same time. I won't have any money—just
a knapsack probably, but I know I have to go, Lucretia. I know I have to get away from this goddamn
place—not you—here! And . . . and even if I stayed
. . . even if I did . . . you know it would be im-
possible, don't you?

LUCRETIA. Briton . . . don't . . . don't say no more,
please?

(*He crosses to bed, sits facing Down Stage. She crosses
to him, and he lays his head against her belly.
The lights fade out. LOU enters the porch in darkness, and GREMMAR enters to foot of bed. The
lights rise in a special on GREMMAR and on LOU,
as LOU sits on the bench. NATE moves slowly up
to porch from Stage Left. GREMMAR exits Up
Stage Right.*)

NATE. What's up? (LOU *shrugs.*) Everybody in bed?
(LOU *nods, as* NATE *moves onto the porch.*) Oh brother,
I thought it would have cooled off a little by now anyway! (*He is silent a moment and then turns his head
toward* LOU. *He speaks softly because of the lateness
of the hour. His tones are suggestive rather than
angry.*) Lou, man, I'm telling you. (*Shaking his head.*)

LOU. (*Turning, looking at him.*) Telling me what?

NATE. (*Shrugging, pause.*) Tonight . . . All that
carrying on in there—

LOU. (*Tense.*) What do you mean "carrying on?"

NATE. (*Slight pause.*) All that . . . testifying, crying and falling out nonsense. Man, come off that stuff,
will you? That's . . . old folk's bullshit . . . breaking down all over the place and acting like asses!—

LOU. (*Defensively.*) I couldn't help it, Nate! I—I
wasn't . . . trying to! . . . It just . . . happened,

that's all! . . . I can't help it if you don't believe in
it! . . . I do—all right?

NATE. I didn't say I didn't believe in it, man. You
just don't have to get so carried away with it, that's
all. Shit, you can do all the believing you damn well
please, but it still doesn't call for all them shenanigans.
No indeed!

LOU. (*Rises and crosses Down Stage.*) Look, Nate,
let's drop it! . . . It's my business! . . . If— If I'm
supposed to be ashamed of myself, then I'm not! . . .
You just do what you want, and I'll do what I want!—

NATE. (*Crosses to bench and sits.*) So be an ass—
all right? . . . Maybe you should've seen yourself.
(LOU *turns partly toward* NATE, *speaking with extreme
difficulty, tension, yet softly.*)

LOU. Nate . . . you know what? . . . I . . . I . . .
I really think there's . . . something wrong with me
—I really do.

NATE. (*Turning slowly, frowning.*) What do you
mean?

LOU. I . . . I don't know . . . There's something
wrong . . .

NATE. What do you mean you don't know? You just
said there was something wrong with you, so what the
hell are you talking about?

LOU. (*Crosses to bench and sits Stage Left.*) It's
just that . . . Last week . . . Peggy and I, well, we
went out . . . parking, you know . . . in the woods
. . . near Martin's Dam . . . and, well, we were there
and . . . one thing led to another, and . . . we started
fooling around—

NATE. Well that's not it is it? What the hell's wrong
with that?

LOU. I'm not finished.

NATE. Because I was going to say, man—

LOU. We started . . . fooling around . . . all that
stuff, and, well, you know . . . she wanted me to . . .
you know? . . . I guess I wanted to . . . I guess . . .

(*Pause.*) So . . . when it was time . . . even before
it was time . . . before . . . she took my hand and
put it . . . down there . . . and . . . I got sick . . .
I got sick! . . . I vomited! I just . . . puked all over
the place! . . . I just all of a sudden got this . . .
sick feeling in the pit of my stomach, and . . . and
it all came up—and I just couldn't do it! I couldn't!
. . . I don't know what was wrong—why I got so
sick—

NATE. (*Laughing.*) So you got sick—so what?

LOU. (*Angrily.*) What do you mean "so what?" I
threw up!— (LOU *crosses Down Stage Left.*)

NATE. Tell me the honest to god's truth, Lou—have
you ever had any nookie before? (LOU *doesn't answer,
turning away.* NATE *rises and crosses.*) I know you
ain't—knowing you, you haven't. Shit, there's nothing
wrong with you, nigger—not a damn thing! . . . Shit,
I know your problem. Shit, man, you just have to get
on that stuff and just start working out! Work out,
nigger and don't ask no questions—don't even think
about it, brother. Just get on it and get the job done!
That's your problem, man. You think too much about
it! Just let nature take over and forget all that . . .
fiery furnace stuff. Stuff'll mess you up every time,
when you want some of it. Indeed it will! I'm sorry,
but that's just not the time for it. Hell, worry about it
after you've busted your nuts. Get guilty later, if you
want to. It'll pass, believe you me, it will pass! Just
get on it and knock that shit out and chalk it up, and
square it with your conscience later—much later, if
that's what's bothering you. (*Sits Down Stage Center
on edge of porch.*) Yeah, be ready for that stuff when
it comes, man because sometimes it's far and few between! Indeed!

LOU. (*Speaking softly but intensely.*) Nate . . .
some—sometimes I get . . . I get so sick and tired of
it all! . . . I really do! . . . Honest to God!

NATE. What's that—nookie? Shit! I don't . . . I
don't never get tired of it man—never!—

LOU. Sometimes I'd . . . I'd like to . . . to . . .
take a knife and . . . and just . . . rip this black
stuff off!—just . . . skin myself clean! I—

NATE. You'd just bleed, man, that's all . . . just
bleed . . . (NATE *rises after a moment, and then goes
up to* LOU *and claps him on the shoulder, shaking him
gently.*) Ease up, man . . . just ease up! . . . Fuck
it, you know? I mean, just plain fuck it all! . . . Just
keep moving and you don't get hurt . . . And don't let
some of it hang out, let it all! You know what I mean?
(NATE *puts his arm around his shoulder.*) Fuck it—
Just plain fuck it all! You know? (*Lights begin slow
fade.*)

LOU. (*Sighing heavily, shrugging.*) Yeah . . .
yeah . . .

(*Lights out and curtain falls medium; during Act
    Break No. 2 Wall is flown out to reveal No. 3
    Wall for* HARPER *flashback.*)

ACT TWO

Curtain rises— Medium— It is Saturday afternoon. The set is the same except for a table cloth on the dining table. The Bible, cup and saucer, and tray have been struck. The bed upstairs has been made up.

At rise, LOU *is sitting on floor of porch at the entrance to the house reading a biology book.* MILTON *and* NATE *are Down Stage of desk in living room discussing a bid for a plastering job.*

NATE. Pop, the bid is way too low, for Pete's sake!

MILTON. Nathan, you don't have to get greedy about it!

NATE. Who's getting greedy! Pop, the trouble with you is you always bid too low!

MILTON. Look, Nathan, I got it figured down right here! That's why I called you in here!

NATE. Pop, you don't have a thing here for—for profit—not a thing! . . . for time and aggravation!

MILTON. Nathan, that house isn't going to take anymore than two weeks!

NATE. Pop, by the time we buy material, pay everybody, what do we have left?

MILTON. (*Giving the bid to* NATE.) Nathan, look at these figures down there again, will you?

NATE. I'm looking at them! All they're saying is that we're going to have to scramble and charge at the lumber yard for the next job, instead of charging what the job is worth. (*Crosses Stage Center.*) You always underbid because you're afraid of not getting the job!

MILTON. (*Steps to* NATE.) I charge what the job is

worth, and that's what I've been doing all these years!—

NATE. And that's why we don't have any capital now!

MILTON. (*Crosses Stage Right.*) I've been able to provide for this family, haven't I? Nobody's in need of anything here, are they?

NATE. (*Steps to* MILTON.) Pop, just tell me—why do we always have to submit the lowest bid, huh? No wonder we always get the job. They know they're going to get a first class job for the least amount of money. Those white contractors, they see us coming, and they laugh all the way to the bank. (*Crosses Stage Center.*) As far as I'm concerned—

MILTON. (*Grabbing the bid again and studying it.*) All right, all right, let me see the paper. (*Sits at desk and opens ledger, which is on desk.*)

NATE. I'd rather risk not getting the job than to— Things are going up, and here we are charging the same thing we did last year. That house has got—

(JOE DRAKE *moves up to walk on to the porch from Stage Left.*)

DRAKE. Hello, Nate.

LOU. (*Rising quickly, polite, but attempting to mask the indignation at the mistake.*) I'm not . . . Nate . . .

DRAKE. Oh, I'm sorry . . . I—I thought you were. (DRAKE *forces a smile.*) Is . . . your father in? . . . It's Joe Drake.

LOU. (*Moving toward the porch door.*) Just a minute . . . (*Going to* MILTON.) Pop, it's Joe Drake. (NATE *crosses Up Stage at desk hovers over* MILTON.)

MILTON. Tell him I'll be there in a minute—I'm finishing up on the bid. (*Gestures for* NATE *to sit;* NATE *sits anxiously on the piano stool.*)

LOU. (*Returning to porch.*) He'll be here in a second. (DRAKE *stands hesitantly.*) Won't you have a seat?

DRAKE. Thank you. (*He sits Stage Right on bench.* LOU *crosses Stage Left and sits on floor. Throughout the scene with* DRAKE, LOU *tries to be polite, though he is somewhat ill-at-ease.*) You must be Lou then? (LOU *nods, grinning somewhat shyly.*) Your father and Nate are good plasterers. (*Pause.*) That Nate is the best I've ever seen—a first class perfectionist! I have work, I try to make certain they get it.— So, how's school going?

LOU. (*Reluctantly, shrugging.*) Okay . . . so far . . .

DRAKE. (*Nodding, pause.*) Your brother tells me you want to be a doctor some day.

LOU. (*Looking directly at him.*) I hope so . . .

DRAKE. Well that's great . . . that's great . . . Who knows, may be some day I'll be getting a checkup from you. (*He laughs, pausing as* LOU *forces a polite smile.*) My kid's in school too— Yale . . . Every once in a while he sends me stuff home to read— things he's been studying . . . Wants to make sure I don't get too complacent—wants some intelligent conversation when he comes home on vacations . . . doesn't want a dunce as a father. (*Laughing again.* LOU *is stoic.*) Your . . . father tells me you don't like plastering very much . . .

LOU. (*Softly, hesitantly.*) It's . . . all right . . .

DRAKE. Well, it's hard work . . .

LOU. I'd just . . . rather be doing . . . something else—

DRAKE. Well I don't blame you, son—no, I don't . . . I don't blame my own kid for not wanting to go into the building business. No, let him make up his own mind what he wants to be—

MILTON. (*Turns to* NATE.) All right, seventeen hundred— (*Rises.*)

NATE. (*Rises.*) It's still not enough!

MILTON. (*Crosses Stage Right.*) Nathan, I can't charge that man no more than that!—

NATE. (*Following.*) Drake's got it.

MILTON. Now you're being ridiculous!

NATE. It ought to be at least two thousand!

MILTON. Nathan, I'm sorry, but I'm just not going to do it!

NATE. That old place has got closets and pipes galore—

MILTON. I know what it's got! I can see! I'm not going to charge Drake any two thousand, so you may as well stop!—

NATE. Well I don't know why you asked my opinion in the first place.

MILTON. (*Crossing Stage Center.*) Nathan, I appreciate your help, but I thought you'd use better sense.

NATE. Well maybe you'd better figure out the bids yourself from now on! (*He angrily crosses Down Stage Right, sits in arm chair. MILTON stops, looks at him for a moment, and then studies the bid. Going to the table, he writes a figure on it and steps to NATE.*)

MILTON. All right, I got it up to eighteen hundred, but I certainly can't charge the man any more than that—absolutely not! (*Crosses to porch.*)

NATE. (*Without looking up.*) Pop, it's your business . . .

MILTON. (*Appearing at the door.*) Hello, Mr. Drake, I'm sorry to keep you waiting.

DRAKE. (*Rises.*) Oh no, that's all right. Your boy and I were just out here talking.

MILTON. Come on into the living room, Mr. Drake, where it's more comfortable. It's so hot out here.

DRAKE. (*Following him.*) Okay. Nice talking to you, Lou. (*The two men go into the living room. DRAKE sees NATE.*) How are you doing, Nate?

NATE. (*Sullenly.*) Okay, Mr. Drake, how are you?

DRAKE. Oh fair to middling. (*Sitting at table, Stage Left.*)

MILTON. (*Handing him the bid and then sitting opposite him.*) I tried to make it as fair as I could.

DRAKE. (*Putting on a pair of glasses.*) Oh I know that—I know that. Just let me take a quick gander at it. I'm sure it'll be all right. (*He looks at the bid and then frowns.*) Milton . . . this is a little high, isn't it?

MILTON. Mr. Drake, like I said, I tried to be fair.

DRAKE. (*Re-examining the bid.*) I'm sure you did, but—

MILTON. And I'm still not making any money . . . Material's gone up. I've got my men to pay, and they have to get union scale—

DRAKE. My expenses are up too, Milton.

MILTON. I have to make some money, Mr. Drake. Both of us are after some kind of profit—

DRAKE. Agreed, Milton, but it's just that your other bids were so much lower.

MILTON. I really didn't charge what I should have then.

DRAKE. I thought you said it would take two weeks. Here you have three—

MILTON. Mr. Drake, I don't like to rush things. I want to give you a first-class job—

DRAKE. And you always do, but—

MILTON. There's a lot to be done in that house, Mr. Drake—

DRAKE. Milton, you know I have other bids?

MILTON. I'm aware of that.

DRAKE. (*Pause.*) This one is pretty steep. Milton, you know I'm not trying to beat you out of money —you know that?

MILTON. Well I certainly hope you wouldn't.

DRAKE. Well I wouldn't . . . And I really would like you and Nate to have this job because you do such damned good work. (*Looking slowly at the bid again.*) But . . . on the basis of this . . . I . . . I really have to consider some of the others.

MILTON. (*Shrugging.*) Well I'm sorry, Mr. Drake . . . I gave you the figures I . . .

DRAKE. You wouldn't consider dropping it a little, would you? Sixteen hundred—how does that sound?

MILTON. Mr. Drake, I already gave you what I thought—

DRAKE. (*Rises, crosses Down Stage of table to stand between* MILTON *and* NATE.) Milton, I'm trying to arrive at something equitable for both of us—so both of our purposes can be served. I really want you and Nate to have the job, and that's no joke! Sixteen hundred—no higher, no less. (MILTON *is silent, thinking.* NATE *watches anxiously.*)

MILTON. Let me see the bid.

DRAKE. I'm not trying to pressure you now— (*Handing him the bid and crossing Up Center behind table.*)

MILTON. (*Studying the bid.*) You're not pressuring me.

DRAKE. Sixteen hundred.

MILTON. Sixteen hundred?

DRAKE. Sixteen. . . .

MILTON. (*A lengthy pause.*) All right . . . but . . . Lord knows I can't do it any cheaper.

DRAKE. I'm not asking you to. Sixteen hundred. We have a deal then? (*Offering his hand, which* MILTON *shakes.*) Good. Have it typed up, and we'll both sign it. I'm really glad we could compromise, Milton. You guys have me spoiled when it comes to your work. (*Looking at his watch.*) Okay then . . . I've got to get out of here. The wife and I are having some friends over tonight, and if I'm not back on time, she'll hit the roof. (MILTON *follows him to the door.* NATE *disgustedly crosses Up Stage to desk.*) When do you think you can get started, Milton?

MILTON. Oh . . . Monday, I suppose . . .

DRAKE. Good . . . sounds good. (*Looking for* NATE, *who is out of view.*) Okay, Milton, I'll be talking to you a little later in the week, all right?

MILTON. All right.

DRAKE. (*Shaking his hand again.*) Goodnight, Milton.

MILTON. Goodnight. (DRAKE *moves onto the porch, leaving* MILTON *in the living room studying the bid again.*)

DRAKE. Goodnight, Lou. Lots of luck in school, son.

LOU. (*Softly.*) Thank you.

(DRAKE *leaves, Stage Left.* MILTON *moves into the living room and sits at the table, Stage Left.* NATE *turns and glares at him.*)

NATE. Pop, you had him! Why did you let that man beat you down?—

MILTON. Now, Nathan, nobody beat nobody—

NATE. Pop, he most certainly did! (*Hearing* NATE's *loud repsonses,* LOU *rises and moves into the living room and sits in Stage Left arm chair, listening.*)

MILTON. Nathan, I got a hundred dollars more than I started with! Now we can at least be thankful for that!—

NATE. Pop, you were asking for eighteen hundred, not sixteen! Maybe that's how that man can afford to send his son to Yale—by beating us down!

MILTON. Nathan—

NATE. You had him! You should've just told him to go and get somebody else if he didn't like it! Who needs— (*Turns Stage Right.*)

MILTON. (*Rises and crosses Up Stage Center.*) Nathan, you don't know anything about bargaining. In business sometimes you have to compromise. Now you know that—

NATE. Oh for goodness sakes, Pop, if that white man had asked for nine hundred, he'd have beaten you into less than that!

MILTON. I wouldn't have done anything of the kind! I'm getting sick and tired of you telling me what I'm supposed to do with white people!—

NATE. Maybe if you'd just listen to me just once—just once!

MILTON. I've been dealing with these people longer than you were born! And you're trying to tell me! (*Pacing, ranting.*) Took my trowel long before you were born! Brought it across that man's face— Jake Ricker—man calling me out of my name! Jumped on him and beat him to the floor—slurring me—the white devil! Beat him down! And you trying to tell me about white people!—

NATE. I'm giving you my opinion—all right?

MILTON. I didn't ask you for any opinion! I know what you're calling me!

NATE. Oh let's just forget it—forget it! I'm trying to tell you how I feel! If you don't appreciate it then—

MILTON. I don't want to know how you feel! . . . I'm trying to feed and clothe you—I don't want to hear another word! I don't want you to bat an eye around here from now on! (*Pacing.*) Here I am trying to work and keep my dignity—I'm spending a year in jail beating up that man . . . learning to keep my dignity —keep my reputation—and I have to get some smart lip from you! I'm surprised at you, Nathan! You ought to be ashamed of yourself! Well I don't want to hear another word! (MILTON *turns, sees* LOU, *and crosses to him.* LOU *rises and backs on to the porch.* GREMMAR, *who has heard the noise, starts down the stairs, carrying the scrabble game.*) And you are working for me this summer, young man—as long as I need some help—next summer too, whether you're willing or not! You don't have nothing to say about it! I'm your father, and you are going to respect me! You hear me? (GLORIA *appears at the porch, interrupting* MILTON'*s tirade.* GREMMAR *moves toward the porch, but stops just inside living room entrance.*) Can I help you? (LOU *crosses Up Stage on porch behind bench.*)

GLORIA. Mr. Edwards?

MILTON. Yes?

GLORIA. I'm Gloria Townes . . . Tom's wife.

MILTON. Yes?

GLORIA. Can—can I talk with you a minute?

MILTON. (*Pause, frowning.*) Would . . . would you like to come in?

GLORIA. (*Glancing nervously at* LOU.) No, I . . . I . . . (*Pause.*)

MILTON. (*Looking strangely at her.*) What—what can I do for you, Mrs. Townes?

GLORIA. Well . . . (*Again looking at* LOU.) Could I . . . could I . . . see you down here a minute!

MILTON. Please come inside Mrs. Townes. (GLORIA *enters living room, nodding to* GREMMAR *as she passes.* MILTON *follows.* GREMMAR *goes to porch and sits on bench with* LOU *to play scrabble.*)

GLORIA. (*Standing Up Center behind table.*) I don't have much time, Mr. Edwards, I just come over for Tom's pay.

MILTON. (*Behind Stage Right arm chair.*) His what?

GLORIA. I said, his pay, Tom says you haven't given him his pay—the last three weeks before you laid him off, you haven't given that man nothing!

MILTON. Oh now, Mrs. Townes!—

GLORIA. And that's not right!

MILTON. (*Crosses to* GLORIA.) Mrs. Townes, I'm a deacon in the church now—

GLORIA. Mr. Edwards, you shouldn't be hiring nobody if you can't afford to pay them— (LOU *and* GREMMAR *stop playing to listen to the conversation.*)

MILTON. Mrs. Townes, your husband is lying—

GLORIA. My husband hasn't got no right to lie to me—

MILTON. I paid Tom every cent he earned—every cent!—

GLORIA. Well he said—

MILTON. And some days he wouldn't even show up, and I'm depending on him—

GLORIA. Mr. Edwards, I think it's a shame for

colored people to treat other colored people the way
you're treating my husband—

MILTON. Mrs. Townes, why would I want to cheat
Tom, huh?—

GLORIA. I don't know! That's up to you to answer.
All I know is—

MILTON. The man coming to work drunk half the
time—half can't do his work—

GLORIA. (*Her voice rising.*) I beg your pardon! I beg
your pardon! Tom hasn't never left my house drunk—
hasn't never! Mr. Edwards, if you have the money, I'd
appreciate having it. My children's get colds, I'm
running out of things. We are poor negroes, Mr. Edwards—

MILTON. Now wait a minute—wait just a minute!
I want to show you something here! (*Moving quickly
to the desk to get the ledger.*) Isn't that something?

GLORIA. It's a shame!—a damn shame!— It's awful!
(MILTON *crosses to the table, carrying the ledger; puts
it on the table and attempts to show it to her.*)

MILTON. Every cent! My boy Nathan puts it in here
promptly every week—doesn't miss a one. Now look
here, Mrs. Townes—

GLORIA. (*Turning away.*) Mr. Edwards, Tom needs
his money!

MILTON. (*Turning to the payroll section of the
ledger.*) I'm trying to show you, woman. Look—here
it is! I have to pay taxes! You think I want the gov-
ernment down on my back?

GLORIA. Mr. Edwards, I ain't hardly interested in
reading no book!—

MILTON. You want to know the truth, don't you?
(*Pointing to the page.*) Here's the last week the man
worked—right here!—all his pay! And the week before that . . . and before that. It's all in here! Now,
if you don't want to believe that, then I feel sorry for
you! (MILTON *crosses Stage Right.*) Right in here!
(*She reluctantly looks, as* MILTON *crosses back to table*

and points to the page again.) Right there!—and there —and right there!—I'm not trying to cheat your husband, Mrs. Townes. (*She looks closely at the page.*) And then coming up to this house—my house—and throwing a brick through my window because my boy Nate wouldn't lend him some money—drunk!

GLORIA. (*Stunned, steps to* MILTON.) Tom did?

MILTON. Yes, ma'am—that's right!

GLORIA. (*Softly.*) He didn't get laid off?

MILTON. Indeed he did not! . . . I had to fire your husband! (*She is silent, fighting back tears.*) Did Tom send you up here, Mrs. Townes?

GLORIA. (*After a moment, softly, her voice breaking slightly.*) No . . . I . . . I . . . just come . . .

MILTON. Well I'm sorry you did . . . He should've told you not to . . . I'm sorry . . . (*She stands for a moment, sighing heavily and resisting the desire to cry. Turning, she hurries out, exiting Stage Left off the porch.*)

GLORIA. That bastard! (GREMMAR *rises and enters living room.*)

MILTON. (*Standing, looking after her.*) Isn't that something? . . . Tom's nothing but a fool!—nothing but a plain fool!

GREMMAR. (*Crosses to* MILTON.) Milton, I don't want to meddle now—I never did do that with you children—but why don't you give the woman a few dollars—just a couple. She's in trouble, son—

MILTON. Momma, I feel sorry for the woman, but—

GREMMAR. It's not her fault, Milton. I'm not taking the blame off him, but the Lord will deal harshly with him. She does have some little children. Be charitable, Milton. You know the Bible talks about being charitable to others. Others, son. Go on over there, or send one of the boys and just give her a little present. It doesn't have to be much—just a little present. She'll appreciate it. She will. Remember your bible, son. Remember it, and trust in it . . . Trust in it . . .

MILTON. (*After pausing thoughtfully, nods his head.*) I'll do it myself Momma.

(*They both move to porch, and* MILTON *exits Stage Left.* GREMMAR *looks after him, her thoughts again turning inward; lights fade to special on* GREMMAR. *The lights rise simultaneously in* LUCRETIA'S *room as the special fades out.* GREMMAR *and* LOU *clear Stage Left.* LUCRETIA *enters.* HARPER *follows from Up Stage Right, as she puts her purse on dresser.* HARPER *puts his hat on.*)

LUCRETIA. You have to go now, Harper?

HARPER. Yes, ma'am . . . Have to go to work in the morning.

LUCRETIA. What time do you have to be up?

HARPER. Oh, four o'clock thereabouts . . .

LUCRETIA. You have to be down in the mines at four o'clock?

HARPER. Round about then . . . four . . . four-thirty.

LUCRETIA. Lord, at four o'clock I won't be thinking about waking up, unless Little Sam or Edna does it.

HARPER. Yeah, well, it's . . . early all right—it's early. Can't say I like it, but that's when my shift has to go down.

LUCRETIA. (*Crosses to* HARPER.) Well you can stay a bit longer if you want. It won't be imposing on me none. Mrs. Darden, my landlady's got the children for the evening, and she don't mind keeping 'em as long as it's not too late. You sure you won't stay a minute?

HARPER. (*Shyly.*) All right . . . if—if it won't be imposing too much.

LUCRETIA. (*Crosses, Stage Center.*) Heavens no! I'm always up late. Mrs. Darden says I must be a night-owl or something, my light's on so much. (*Pulls chair Down Stage Center.*) Have a sit-down, and I'll be right with you. (*Takes his hat, goes to the dresser and takes off her hat; puts both on dresser.*) I want to thank you for taking me to the services down at the church tonight. Harper, I really enjoyed it.

HARPER. You're certainly welcome. (*She primps at the dresser, catching him staring admiringly at her. He smiles bashfully, dropping his glances.*)

LUCRETIA. You like my beads, Harper? . . . Pretty, aren't they?

HARPER. Yes they are . . . yes . . .

LUCRETIA. Thank you. My husband gave them to me before he passed on—Sam Green? I hope you don't mind me mentioning his name.

HARPER. No, ma'am, go right ahead.

LUCRETIA. He was good to me, Sam was . . . Yes he was. (*Moving away to bed and sitting opposite him.*) There now, I feel better now that I freshened up a bit. (*She smiles, and he shyly returns it.*) A woman should freshen up as much as she can . . . One thing I can't stand is a woman who don't keep herself cleaned up and looking nice. Of course, they get jealous of you if you do—swearing you're trying to steal their menfolk—but it's just being jealous, that's all. (*She smiles again, pleased at herself, a silence following.*) Would you like some tea or something? . . . Won't be no trouble. I usually have some this time of night . . . Helps me to stay awake. I just hate to go to sleep at nights, it seems. I don't get company that often—gets kind of lonesome for a widow like me. (*She rises.*) You're welcome to have some.

HARPER. No thank you . . . I—I appreciate the offer.

LUCRETIA. (*Pause, as she sits back on the bed.*) How . . . how's your studying for the ministry coming along now, Harper?

HARPER. Fine, just fine . . .

LUCRETIA. (*Pause.*) Reverend Lockwood going to make you a preacher soon?

HARPER. Well . . . I preach my trial sermon and

. . . and he says I'll be just about ready. (*Pleased.*)

LUCRETIA. You—you have a church all lined up when you finish your practicing?

HARPER. Reverend Lockwood says he get me one over in Greensborough—folks over there, they needs somebody.

LUCRETIA. Lord Jesus, you must be excited, aren't you?

HARPER. Yeah . . . yeah, I guess I am . . . Yeah . . . it's . . . it's kinda scary, a little. One day I'm just a man way down in the mines, mining coal . . . wasn't even thinking about religion hardly—just making a living—hating it—hating it! And the next day I'm hearing the call of the Lord—hearing it as clear as I'm hearing you now—

LUCRETIA. What'd it sound like?

HARPER. Just as . . . as clear as a bell!—and pretty —just as pretty! The voice of the Lord is sweet! . . . And it's saying to me—saying to me: "I need you, Harper Edwards, to do my will—to preach the gospel —my gospel! I need you!" Well I'm thinking at first— I'm going crazy or something, and I'm trying to shut it out!—

LUCRETIA. Ain't that something!—

HARPER. "Go 'way from here, I'm saying,—go 'way!" But it wouldn't. Kept after me—a couple of weeks, I guess. And . . . well . . . here I am . . . ready to preach and do his will . . . a shepherd looking after his own flock . . . Yeah, I—I get kinda tense when I think about it.

LUCRETIA. Oh Harper, you're going to be a good preacher—I know you will!

HARPER. Well . . . I'm going to do my best, Miss Lucretia—with the help of God.

LUCRETIA. Sure you will . . . (*Pause as she rises and steps to the mirror and primps.*) You . . . you go on over there to Greensborough, and I bet I won't be seeing you no more, I bet, will I?

HARPER. (*With difficulty.*) I—I was going . . . I
was going to . . . to ask you . . . I—

LUCRETIA. Ask me what?

HARPER. Well . . . if . . . if I could come a-court-
ing—

LUCRETIA. Oh Harper—isn't that lovely! That's
lovely! Of course you can!—

HARPER. You're a fine woman, Miss Lucretia—

LUCRETIA. Oh Harper, I haven't done nothing special.
I'm . . . I'm just a . . . a widow trying to look after
her children with the little bit of money her husband
left her—that's all.

HARPER. Well you been doing a fine job—yes, ma'am
. . . Little Sam's a fine-looking boy—a fine looking
lad! And Miss Edna's just as pretty as a picture—

LUCRETIA. (*Crosses to the foot of the bed and sits,
facing audience.*) I done my best, Harper—with the
Lord's help. He's watched over us. Yes he has, ever
since I come here—the kids too young for me to work
much, and hardly no women's jobs at all in this little
mining town. He's made it possible for me and the
children to make it some how on the little bit of sav-
ings I had.

HARPER. Well, a man—especially if he's going to be
a preacher—needs a fine woman—somebody who's
gonna be an inspiration to his soul and light to his path
and his children's path. And—and I been praying a
long time, Miss Lucretia. And I see you at the church
. . . and the Lord spoke to me and told me . . . the
same voice I heard in the mine—told me as clear as
a bell—you was the one.

LUCRETIA. That's so kind of you, Harper. (*Pleased.*)
I know the children are wild about you. Yes they are!
They know a good man when they see one. (*Both
laugh softly, nervously and are silent, groping for
words.*)

HARPER. (*Pleased with himself.*) Well I best be
going . . . I—I done stayed past my time.

LUCRETIA. I'm not sleepy if that's what's troubling you. But . . . if you have to go, since you have to be up so early.

HARPER. Yes, ma'am—four o'clock.

LUCRETIA. Lord, I'm telling you—four o'clock!

HARPER. (*Rising and standing awkwardly.*) Well . . .

LUCRETIA. (*Also standing.*) I want to thank you again for the time at the church, Harper. It was real nice.

HARPER. You're more than welcome, Miss Lucretia —more than welcome.

HARPER. Well goodnight . . . (HARPER *crosses, Stage Right.*)

LUCRETIA. Aren't—aren't you going to . . . kiss me goodnight, Harper? (HARPER *stops and turns to* LU-CRETIA. *She reacts quickly to his being taken aback.*) You can . . . we're courting now, aren't we? You're going to court a woman, you have to learn to kiss her on the cheek or hand or something. (*Holding out her cheek.*) Right there—just a little peck, that's all. (*He does so, shyly.*) There now, that wasn't so bad, was it?

HARPER. (*Smiling.*) Good night . . . Miss Lucretia . . .

LUCRETIA. Your hat, Harper, don't forget it! (*She moves quickly to the dresser and gets the hat and places it on his head, simultaneously kissing him. He exits Up Stage Right, stunned. She laughs gaily. BLACKOUT. In blackout* LUCRETIA *clears Stage Left.* GREMMAR *and* LOU *get into place as the lights rise again on the porch; a special on* GREMMAR. MILTON *enters from Stage Left, the special goes out on* GREM-MAR.)

GREMMAR. You get it straightened out with her, baby?

MILTON. Yeah . . . yeah . . . couldn't help feeling sorry for the woman though . . . (GREMMAR *begins coughing suddenly—heavy, wracking coughing.*) Do

. . . do you feel all right, Momma? (*Sitting beside her as* Lou *stands, equally concerned.*)

GREMMAR. (*Slowly.*) Oh I'm all right, son . . . just a little headache . . . a little one . . . The heat, I guess . . . I'm a little tired . . . Probably should go on upstairs and rest some . . No sir, can't do like I use to . . . not like I use to . . .

MILTON. Oh Momma, you're still as spry as—

GREMMAR. (*Decisively.*) Oh no . . . no . . . no, sir . . . No, I can't lie to myself . . . Not going to do me one bit of good . . . No, son, I'm not a young woman no more . . . I know the road . . . Momma used to recite a poem to me. She used to say:

"Oh, the old sheep, they know the road,
    The old sheep, they know the road.
    The old sheep, they know the road;
    Young lambs must find the way."

Yes, the young lambs must find the way . . . I know the road . . . Well let me get up from here with this scrabble and go upstairs for a while . . . A little rest may help me. (MILTON *helps* GREMMAR *to her feet, and she crosses into living room with* MILTON *and* Lou *following.*) You all don't bother about waiting for me for dinner. I'll eat something a little later on.

MILTON. Put the fan on up there, Momma. Louis, help her upstairs, will you? (Lou *rises crosses to* GREMMAR, *takes her arm, and they move up the stairs.* MILTON *follows to the foot of the stairs and stands watching—concerned.*)

GREMMAR. The old sheep, they know the road . . . the young lambs must find the way . . . find the way . . . (GREMMAR *stops at the top of stairs, gives the scrabble game to* Lou, *who exits Stage Right. She exits Up Stage Right.* MILTON *returns the ledger to the writing table. He stands, thinking for a moment, he sits at the table Stage Right chair, staring distantly, painfully.* HATTIE *enters from the kitchen and crosses Stage Center.*)

HATTIE. (*Softly.*) Milton, are you all right?

MILTON. (*Sighing.*) Yeah . . . I'm, all right. (*She frowns curiously at him, then begins to remove the table cloth.*)

HATTIE. Milton, I'd like to set the table.

MILTON. (*Turning to look up the stairs, as* HATTIE *is folding table cloth.*) I don't know, Hattie, but . . . everytime I think about . . . (*Pause.*) Momma use to be so . . . active . . . spry . . . cutting up and on the go—going here and there—just had to be doing something—doing something! Busy! . . . It just doesn't seem to . . . make sense! (*Sighing again— pause.*) I look at her now and . . . in some ways . . . she's . . . not even the same person . . . It's . . . somebody else—not Momma . . . somebody else . . . Somebody almost like her, but like a stranger— Somebody that—that reminds me of her . . . Has the same walk . . . same kind of laugh . . . same way of talking, but— (HATTIE *crosses behind* MILTON *and puts her hands on his shoulders.*)

HATTIE. Your mother's not a young woman now, Milton, she—

MILTON. I know, I know. (MILTON *rises, sighing.*) Well I guess I'll go on outside for a while. Weeds are taking over the string beans.

HATTIE. (*Crosses down to a level with* MILTON.) Milton, do you know how hot it is out there?—do you? You'll get yourself a stroke! (*Wiping his brow.*) Look at yourself now—sweating and all! You already worked half the day, plastering! It ought to be enough for you! Sit down and rest and be sensible! You're not one of the boys!

MILTON. I use to . . . use to be able to work out there in that heat when I was younger . . . didn't think nothing of it—

HATTIE. Well you certainly aren't younger now!—

MILTON. Momma would—would come all the way out to me . . . a mile near . . . worrying about me, trying to get me to slow down or stop. "Sun can't hurt me, Momma—can't hurt me!" Always so worried about me.

HATTIE. Milton, you can't stop living now. If I'd stopped the day I realized my mother and father were old people, I'd be no more good today. Now, all of us, if the Lord spares us, has to grow old and leave this world, and your Momma's one of them. So just make up your mind to it. Besides, there's nothing more beautiful than somebody that's grown old as gracefully as that woman has.

MILTON. (*Turns to* HATTIE.) Yeah, I suppose you're right.

HATTIE. If you're a Christian, I'm right.

MILTON. You're right, you're right, Hattie.

HATTIE. I know I'm right.

(*They hug.* HATTIE *picks up the center piece,* MILTON *the table cloth. As they exit to kitchen,* MILTON *repeats: "The old sheep they know the road; young lambs must find a way." BLACKOUT to denote passage of time. As lights rise on the porch and living room,* GREMMAR *enters from Down Stage Left, wearing a straw hat and carrying the garden spade. She crosses into living room, but suddenly suffers a dizzy spell, Stage Center. She pauses, regaining her composure, and crosses to piano, putting her hat and spade on top of piano, and sitting on the stool. As she does,* LOU, NATE *and* HOPE *enter from kitchen carrying a birthday cake, a pitcher with punch, and glasses. They are singing happy birthday. As* LOU *and* NATE *hug* GREMMAR, HOPE *lights the candles, and* HATTIE *and* MILTON *enter from kitchen.*)

LOU. (*Joined by* NATE *and* HOPE.) Speech—speech!

GREMMAR. (*Crosses to Up Stage Center and sits at*

table.) Oh now, you all didn't have to go to all this trouble!—

MILTON. Wasn't any trouble, Momma— (EDNA *enters slowly from Stage Right, down the stairs carrying a gift wrapped package.*)

GREMMAR. And me looking a mess!—

NATE. (*Teasing.*) That's all right, Gremmar, you're among kinfolk.

GREMMAR. Well I want to thank you—all of you. Thank you so much.

EDNA. (*Crosses to* GREMMAR *and gives her a gift.*) Happy Birthday, Momma! (*As they exchange kisses.*)

GREMMAR. Thank you, baby. When'd you get here? Nobody told me.

EDNA. Couldn't spoil the surprise, Momma. Anyway, you was out in the garden just a piddling and poking around.

GREMMAR. Well it's good to see you, baby—yes it is. (*Seeing* HOPE.) Lord what a pretty face. How are you, dear?

HOPE. Fine, Mrs. Edwards. Happy Birthday. (HOPE *gives* GREMMAR *a kiss and then a small gift which she brought in on the tray.*)

GREMMAR. Thank you, sugar.

NATE. Okay, Gremmar, it's time to blow out the candles!

GREMMAR. Lord have mercy, I'm not that old, am I? How many of these things you have on there?

LOU. Just sweet sixteen, Gremmar.

GREMMAR. Oh child, I know that's not true. No, sir —a long time since I was that!

HATTIE. Come on now, Momma, time to blow now.

GREMMAR. Now I know I'm not that big a bag of wind, am I? You all trying to tell me something?

EDNA. (*To the laughter of the others.*) You have to try anyway. Come on, Momma. There isn't that many.

GREMMAR. All right . . . lemme see here . . . Where'll I start? . . . All right. (*She blows—*)

(*BLACKOUT, the lights rising upstairs.* LUCRETIA *sits on the bed and* HARPER *in the chair.* LUCRETIA *looks at him with excitement and admiration.*)

LUCRETIA. I keep saying to myself: That's Reverend Edwards— Reverend Edwards!

HARPER. (*Smiling, trying to restrain his joy.*) Yeah . . . yeah, I—I guess that's me all right.

LUCRETIA. Yes, and that was a wonderful sermon you preached for your trial one—a wonderful sermon!

HARPER. Yeah, it felt good . . . yeah . . . After it was all over, Reverend Lockwood grins and says, "Well, looks like you made it son. You're a preacher now!"

LUCRETIA. (*Exuberant, she crosses Down Stage Left of chair to dresser and puts her hat down.*) Lord, you had them folks just a-shouting and carrying on—getting happy! And you were just a preaching on—a preaching on!

HARPER. (*Laughing, pleased.*) Couldn't help myself. The Lord was talking to me.

LUCRETIA. Well he certainly must've been! And—and the collection basket was full up too! Some of them folks was putting in dollar bills! That shows you! Colored folks ain't going to put nothing in the collection basket unless they enjoys it—put in a lot of pennies maybe—

HARPER. (*Pleased.*) Yeah . . . yeah . . . they don't like something, they'll let you know about it one way or another. (*Looking at her with admiration, as she takes his hat and puts it on the dresser, then crosses to bed and sits.*) You was a hit too, little lady—all the folks looking at you—

LUCRETIA. (*Frowning.*) They . . . they were looking at me? (*He nods. They exchange smiles and a lengthy stare.*)

HARPER. Yeah . . . "That man certainly couldn't've done no better for somebody who's going to be a preacher's wife! She's a pretty thing!" (*Laughing nervously.*) They're . . . right about that.

LUCRETIA. (*Crosses to* HARPER.) I—I didn't hear nothing. I—I was so busy watching you after the service—making sure none of those other ladies was trying to steal you. (*Laughing coyly.*)

HARPER. No need to worry about that . . . no . . . ! (*They exchange a lengthy, warm stare. He drops his eyes and rises, crossing Down Stage Right, as* LUCRETIA *crosses Down Stage Left.*) And . . . and one of the members ups to me after the service and says, "That sure is a pretty child, Reverend . . . Use to be a child that looked like that in Roanoke a while back. Belonged to a famly—

LUCRETIA. (*Quickly, fearfully—turning to* HARPER.) I—I've never been to Roanoke—never. I—

HARPER. That's what I told him . . . I couldn't imagine nobody in Roanoke as . . . pretty as you. (*He grins, pleased with his boldness.*)

LUCRETIA. Never in my life . . . (*Crossing to dresser, avoiding contact with him.*) Who—who was this . . . gentleman that was asking?

HARPER. (*Crosses to chair.*) Oh, a short little dark fellow. He's been around White Rock off and on since I been attending. Drops in and out—

LUCRETIA. (*Attempting to collect herself.*) Who—who—what was this girl's name—the one he thought I was?

HARPER. He plum forgot, it's been so long since he's been back there.

LUCRETIA. Oh . . . (*Feigning gaiety.*) Well it couldn't have been me, since I've never been there! Must've been my double or something.

HARPER. "Sure is pretty and familiar-looking pretty." (HARPER *sits, as* LUCRETIA *crosses behind the chair to sit Down Stage on bed.*)

LUCRETIA. Well . . . the next time, thank the gentleman for me. (*Nervously.*) It's—it's been so hot out

. . . seems like . . . we haven't had a breeze all summer. (*Pause, silent, breathing more heavily and reacting nervously to* Harper's *admiring look.*) I . . . I think I hear the children . . . downstairs . . . I think . . . Did—did you hear 'em? Little Sam probably wants me now . . . Edna wakes up because he does. (*He rises reluctantly, and she does also.*)

Harper. Well I best be going . . . It—it don't seem possible I won't be going down in that mine tomorrow . . . I been going down in all that blackness for so long, it just seems strange, you know? . . . Lord knows I'm glad I don't have to . . . you've been a blessing to me, Lucretia. The Lord's done answered my prayers all the way 'round, he has.

Lucretia. (*Sighing heavily.*) Thank . . . thank you, Harper . . . You've been a blessing to me too. Well, I guess I'd better be getting to the children. (*She crosses to dresser and gets his hat.*)

Harper. (*Starting to go, but stopping Stage Right at foot of bed.*) Won't be long before you'll be the good Reverend's wife—

Lucretia. (*Crosses to* Harper.) Yes, yes, that's right . . . I'd better . . . go, Harper. (*Giving the hat to* Harper.) You—you have a good time over there in Greensborough. And—and don't you let none of them pretty-looking sisters over there turn your head now—

Harper. (*Wanting to kiss her fully, but restraining.*) No need to worry about that . . . no need at all. (*Staring at her and then turning to go, his reluctance visible.*) Well . . . goodnight . . .

Lucretia. Harper? (*He stops.*) That—that man—the one that asked you about me?—the girl he thought I was?— Well I'm . . . I'm glad it was me and not her that has you. (*He smiles and then kisses her almost fearfully on the cheek. He looks at her warmly and then leaves. She watches his departure and then turns and crosses Stage Center.*) Never . . . never been to Roanoke in my life—not even near it . . . wouldn't know it if I stumbled over it!

(*As the lights blackout on* LUCRETIA, *exiting Stage
Left, applause is heard, and lights rise on the
living room.* GREMMAR *leans over the candles,
having blown them out. The others are applaud-
ing. She begins to cough slightly.*)

MILTON. You all right Momma?

GREMMAR. (*Feigning.*) I'm all right . . . Just a
little cough . . .

HATTIE. Sit right there, dear, I'll cut the cake for
you.

GREMMAR. After all that huffing and puffing, I need
to.

HATTIE. (*Cutting the cake.*) You all come and help
yourselves. I'm not waiting on nobody but Gremmar
tonight. This is her night! (*They respond, moving to
the table and helping themselves to punch, cake and
the other foodstuffs. After getting various items,* NATE
and HOPE *sit in Stage Left arm chair.* LOU *sits at table
in Stage Left chair.*)

EDNA. (*Crossing between table and stage right arm
chair.*) You don't have any "tea" in here, do you,
Milton?

MILTON. (*Standing behind Stage Right arm chair.*)
Tea? . . . What "tea" are you talking about?

EDNA. The "tea" that makes you high.

MILTON. (*Crosses Down Stage and sits in chair.*)
Girl, you better go 'way from here!

EDNA. (*Laughing along with the others.*) Lord,
Milton would have a fit if some "tea" was in here.

HATTIE. (*Crosses Down Stage of table to Up Stage
Left of* MILTON.) Milton's not fooling nobody. Doctor
Walker told Milton he should take some of that mess
for his cold—said it would help him—and, Lord Jesus,
there wasn't any trouble at all getting that man to take
his medicine.

MILTON. Hattie—

HATTIE. Three o'clock in the morning and Milton's

getting out of bed, creeping downstairs. "Where are you going, Milton, this time of night?" "Have to take my medicine!"

MILTON. Hattie, now why you want to—

HATTIE. Three o'clock! Usually you have to get the law almost to get him to take some medicine! (*Sits on Up Stage arm of Stage Right chair.*)

NATE. (*Teasing.*) I heard him going downstairs.

MILTON. You all know I was just doing what the man told me—

EDNA. Tasting away, huh, Milton? Making sure to get his medicine *on time!* (*He waves away her laughter.* GREMMAR *begins coughing again.*) So how you feel, Momma? Milton says you haven't been feeling too well.

GREMMAR. Oh, I'm all right, baby—just a little cough . . . little cold or something. I'm all right.

EDNA. Well besides that, you're looking good.

GREMMAR. I ought to go up and change this old rag I got on.

MILTON. Momma, you look fine. Stop worrying . . . Momma's always worrying.

EDNA. Well it wouldn't be her if she didn't. (*She crosses Down Stage Left of* LOU.) Well, Louis, Nathan's got his girl friend—where's yours?

LOU. (*Slightly embarrassed.*) Oh I have more important things to do, Aunt Edna.

HOPE. Well I like that, Louis!

LOU. (*As the others laugh, again embarrassed; rising and crossing Up Stage to* HOPE. EDNA *sits in the chair he vacated.*) No, I mean . . . I mean, I have to do a lot of studying if I want to be a doctor . . . or a . . . scientist . . . I mean . . . after I finish up there'll be lots of time . . . Being a doctor's the most important thing right now . . . We need a lot of doctors and things. I mean . . . some day . . .

HOPE. That's right, Lou—try and squirm out of it.

GREMMAR. (*Reaching out to take* LOU's *hand.*) He's

right . . . Yes, plenty of time . . . No need to rush things . . . He's such a handsome boy, the Lord'll send him one when he's ready.

EDNA. Yes, him and Nathan's goodlooking boys—goodlooking!

NATE. I keep telling Mom that.

HATTIE. (*As the others laugh.*) Lord Jesus! Hope, don't pay no attention to Nathan now. He's just showing off!

HOPE. Don't worry, Mrs. Edwards—I don't. (NATE *frowns mockingly at her.*)

EDNA. Yes, goodlooking!

GREMMAR. (*Patting* LOU's *arm. They exchange smiles.*) No, no need to rush . . . no need . . . plenty of time!

(*Lights fade down to special on* GREMMAR. LUCRETIA *enters bedroom from Stage Left and moves chair Up Stage, as lights rise.* HARPER *enters from Up Stage Right, shouting happily.*)

HARPER. I got my church, Lucretia! I got me . . . a . . . church! (*He laughs unrestrainedly, crosses Stage Center and puts his hat on the chair.*) Those folks in Greensborough, they liked me! . . . They . . . they said . . . "You're the one we want, son! You're the one the—*good* Lord sent us!" That's what they said, Lucretia! I got me a church, woman! (*Laughing happily.*)

LUCRETIA. Harper . . . that—that's beautiful— that's beautiful!

HARPER. (*Happy, wanting to let go fully.*) I'm telling you . . . I'm telling you . . . I'm just so . . . tickled . . . I . . . I just want to . . . I just want to holler again!

LUCRETIA. Why don't you just go on?

HARPER. Yeah . . . yeah . . . The Lord won't mind if I holler a little, will he?

LUCRETIA. (*Laughing.*) Of course not! Go ahead, man—holler! (*He lets out a yell.*) Do it again! Feel real good about it, Harper—go ahead! (*He yells again, and then stops. They exchange glances, laughing softly at first. Their laughter begins to build. They rush suddenly toward each other, laughing, holding hands and swinging almost childishly in a circle, dancing. They stop suddenly, continuing to hold hands and stare at each other. They rush suddenly at each other, embracing, kissing, feeling and touching. He starts to break away but cannot, continuing to react to his passions. As they begin to sink slowly toward the floor, the lights fade out and, as they clear, the Stage Left lights rise in the living room, where every one is laughing.* EDNA *takes a piece of cake and crosses Down Stage of table, up to piano.*)

EDNA. Hattie, this is some scrumptious cake, girl! (EDNA *sits on piano stool.*)

HATTIE. Thank you, dear.

MILTON. (*After a slight pause.*) Hired me a white fellow Saturday.

EDNA. Yesterday?— A white man? Lord Jesus! Milton Edwards, my brother, is carrying on some! Going big time! Has it turned around! Got them working for him!

MILTON. (*Restraining his pleasure, crosses to table and puts his plate down.*) Come around looking for work, so I tried him out. (*Crosses Up Stage to* NATE.) Works pretty good, doesn't he, Nate?

NATE. Yeah, at least we don't have to prop him up after lunch like we did Tom.

MILTON. Lord, no! . . . Quiet . . . Don't say much . . . Just does his work . . .

EDNA. (*Rises.*) Maybe he's afraid of you niggers!

MILTON. I wish you wouldn't use that word, Edna.

EDNA. Well that's what we are, aren't we?

MILTON. Well maybe that's what you are!

EDNA. Well whether we are or not, I'm going to have

another piece of cake! (*Going to the table and getting a piece of cake*.) I can't help it if I like to eat. I guess it don't matter. The Lord takes 'em fat, skinny, short and tall. He ain't prejudiced. That's one thing about him.

NATE. (*Rising and taking* HOPE's *hand*.) We have to run over to Hope's house. We'll be right back.

EDNA. Getting tired of us old heads, huh?

NATE. No, we'll be right back—just a couple minutes. Hope's got an errand to tend to.

GREMMAR. All right, you all have a nice walk now.

HOPE. (*As they leave*.) We'll see you later. (*They leave, exiting off the porch.* EDNA *sits in Stage Right arm chair*.)

EDNA. Yes, Lord, I'm telling you! Momma don't come over to see me no more!

MILTON. (*Crosses to stand behind* GREMMAR.) Edna, you know Momma hasn't been well all weekend. I told you that.

EDNA. I don't mean this weekend! I'm talking about before. Kids say to me: "Where's Grandma? How come she don't come over and stay here like she does at Uncle Milton's?" I say: "I don't know, you have to ask her!"

GREMMAR. Oh now, Edna, child—

LOU. She really has been a little tired this weekend like Pop said, Aunt Edna. (GREMMAR *reaches down and pats his hand, holding it*.)

MILTON. And you know you don't have room over there like we have.

EDNA. Burgess died last year. Momma could sleep with me. The kids they can double up. Yes sir, they wouldn't mind for Momma. No, Momma's just got to be with her baby! (*Laughing, a trace of bitterness contained*.)

MILTON. Edna's just messing now.

EDNA. Well Milton, you are the baby of the family!

GREMMAR. Oh child, you know your Momma didn't

play no favorites. Treated all my children equal—even Little Sam before he passed on—

EDNA. Oh no! One of us messed with Milton, and we liked to've got the devil knocked out of us!

MILTON. Edna, Momma use to spank us all!

EDNA. Me, maybe—but not you and Sam much. (*Rising, getting another piece of cake.*) Yes, Jesus. Momma comes home on the weekends, and before I know it, she's gone on back to work.

MILTON. (*Crossing to Stage Left arm chair and sitting.*) Edna's just trying to start something on Momma's birthday—

EDNA. I'm not trying to start nothing, Milton! I'm just wishing she'd come over and visit me a little more than she does! That's all I'm talking about!

GREMMAR. I will, baby, I will . . . Just as soon as I get over this cough—little headache. All right?—

(*Lights fade to specials on* GREMMAR *and* LUCRETIA. HARPER *enters in darkness from Stage Left and drops his coat and tie on floor, Up Stage of dresser. The lights rise fully upstairs.* LUCRETIA *sits on the Stage Left foot of the bed, her clothing awry.* HARPER, *equally dishevelled, sits next to her —Stage Right—his face buried in his hands.*)

LUCRETIA. You shouldn't fault yourself, Harper, you shouldn't—

HARPER. I let him down, that's what I did! I let him down!—

LUCRETIA. Harper, you didn't . . . Harper, you're . . . you're a—a man!

HARPER. I'm a minister! You hear me? I'm a minister!

LUCRETIA. You're a man too!—

HARPER. A weak one—

LUCRETIA. Harper . . . Harper . . . we both—we both have feelings—

HARPER. We only had a couple of weeks to wait—just a couple more!—

LUCRETIA. Oh Harper, what's the difference? A couple of weeks is supposed to make it right? . . . Harper, it just happened! It can't make us wrong the rest of our lives—

HARPER. (*Standing slowly and crossing Stage Center.*) I . . . I went to Greensborough today . . . Lord knows it was a pretty day! Lord knows! The sun . . . just shining . . . birds flying and jack-rabbits running . . . And I'm sitting in that old buggy, and I'm scared. I'm scared, but I'm happy! I'm scared and happy and filled with the . . . (*Turns to* LUCRETIA.) the spirit of God! . . . It's his day . . . and yours too . . . and the children's, because I'm thinking about all of you and just hoping to God those folks'll accept me into their fold—just hoping . . . Scared some . . . And—and I gets there . . . and they're waiting for me . . . just waiting! Can't wait for me to get down to the ground—can't wait—hands reaching for me—starved to hear the word of God, I'm telling you! Just a-thanking, thanking God for sending me to them! (*Turning to face her.*) I just . . . I just got me a church, Lucretia!

LUCRETIA. Harper, I know . . . I know! And . . . and you're going to be a wonderful minister!—

HARPER. (*Turning away.*) No sooner than I leave 'em . . . here I am . . . acting . . . acting like I don't have the first bit of sense, like some—

LUCRETIA. (*Rises and crosses to him.*) Harper, stop it! . . . Stop! . . . Don't—don't make me feel wrong! I'm not going to let you make me feel wrong! . . . I . . . you . . . you were so happy! I looked at your face and you were so . . . so happy!

HARPER. (*He takes* LUCRETIA's *arms and turns; they counter cross.*) Pray with me, Lucretia, and—and ask for his forgiveness. It's a guilty stain against our record, girl, and we have to—have to . . . wipe it clean—

LUCRETIA. Oh Harper! . . . it—it just happened! We—we were just as happy about you getting your church. It—it just happened!

HARPER. (*Sighing.*) Get on your knees with me, Lucretia . . . Will you do that with me?

LUCRETIA. (*Trying to prevent him from assuming a prayerful position.*) Harper, don't—please!

HARPER. Do you want to be banished from the Kingdom, Lucretia? Is that what you want? Do you want his thunder and lightning to . . . to come down here in this room and—and strike us down?—do you?

LUCRETIA. (*Crosses Down Left Center.*) Harper, I don't *want* . . . I don't want to be a part of no kingdom like that!—

HARPER. (*Following, shaking her.*) Don't you say that! Don't you say that to me! You're talking about the Kingdom He called me to lead folks to! That's what you're talking about! Don't you ever say that to me again! We're going to pray—right now—you and me! (*Assuming a prayerful position at foot of bed.*) Our Father, who art in heaven . . . hallowed be thy name . . . Thy kingdom come . . . Thy will be done . . . on earth as it is in heaven . . . Give us this day our daily bread . . .

LUCRETIA. Harper—please!

HARPER. And forgive us our trespasses, as we forgive those who trespass against us—

LUCRETIA. (*Again trying to break his position.*) Harper, we don't have to be doing this—we don't!

HARPER. And lead us not into temptation . . . but deliver us from evil, for thy name's sake—

LUCRETIA. It isn't wrong—it's not! You—you're just making it wrong yourself!

HARPER. For thine is the power and the glory, forever and ever . . . amen. (*He rises quickly, straightening his clothing, and moves and picks up his coat and tie from floor, and his hat from the chair.*)

LUCRETIA. Harper, where are you going? (*He doesn't respond.*) Harper—Harper, you're not . . . leaving me, are you? (*Rushing, grabbing him. He wrenches away.*) Harper, don't be silly! Come on back here please! (*He exits Up Stage Right. She follows as the lights fade out. Lights up in the living room.*)

EDNA. (*Laughing.*) Sometimes . . . sometimes I think the only reason Momma don't come over is because my daddy was *white!* And Milton and Sam had black ones!

(LOU *looks up slowly at* GREMMAR, *his face registering shock. He slowly slides his hand away from hers and glances at her.*)

HATTIE. (*Also looking at* LOU.) Edna . . .

MILTON. (*Rises and angrily crosses Stage Center.*) Now that isn't right, Edna! That's not a nice thing to say to Momma at all!

EDNA. (*As* LOU *turns away in deep thought.*) I'm just teasing Momma . . . He *was* white, wasn't he? Momma knows I was just teasing, don't you, Momma?

GREMMAR. Edna always did like to tease.

MILTON. Just as determined as she can be to spoil Momma's birthday with her foolishness! (MILTON *crosses Stage Left to arm chair.*)

EDNA. Milton—

HATTIE. (*Crosses Up Stage of table to* LOU.) Let's have a good time now, you all . . . (*Looking at* LOU, *who is more absorbed in thought.*) Louis, you want some more to eat? . . . He eats like a bird now.

GREMMAR. You should eat, son. That's how you get your strength now. (*Reaching over and rubbing his arm.*)

LOU. (*Rising suddenly and moving away from the table.*) I—I'm . . . going on the . . . porch for a while . . . It—it's hot in here . . . (*He smiles tautly at* GREMMAR *and then moves out to the porch, where he stands mesmerized.*)

MILTON. (*Crosses to* EDNA.) I certainly wish to

heaven you'd stop your tomfoolery sometimes, Edna.

EDNA. (*Rises and crosses Down Stage of table to Stage Left.*) I don't know why everybody is so down on me. The man was white, wasn't he? Momma knows—

GREMMAR. All right, baby. Momma'll be over her next day off—next weekend—all right?

HATTIE. Momma, why don't you play us a little song. You feel like it?

MILTON. Edna is just jealous!

HATTIE. Milton!

EDNA. Milton knows I'm telling the truth!—

MILTON. (*Crossing to kitchen with* HATTIE *following.*) Why don't you stay home sometime, and don't come over to my house no more!

EDNA. (*Following.*) Now wait a minute! I'll come over and see my momma any time I want to.

GREMMAR. All right, children, don't fuss. Momma's going to play now. (*She goes slowly to the piano and collapses suddenly on the stool. The lights fade to special on* GREMMAR. *Lights also rise in bedroom, as* LUCRETIA *enters from Up Stage Right with a basket of clothes and sits in chair. As she sits,* HARPER *enters from Up Stage Right, where he stands staring icily at* LUCRETIA.)

LUCRETIA. (*Rises and crosses down to level with* HARPER.) Harper—Harper, what's the matter? . . . Don't . . . you feel good? . . . Something happened? (*He continues to stare and then begins toward her, seething, stopping near her.*)

HARPER. You . . . you lied to me, didn't you?

LUCRETIA. I what?

HARPER. You lied to me, didn't you?

LUCRETIA. (*Avoiding his stare.*) Lied?

HARPER. (*Taking a step closer.*) Didn't you?

LUCRETIA. I—I don't know what you're talking about. (*Attempting to pass him.*) I—I better go now . . . the . . . the . . . children—

HARPER. (*Lunging, grabbing her arm and twisting it.*) You tell me the truth!—

LUCRETIA. (*Screaming in pain.*) Harper, you're—my arm, Harper! Harper, what's wrong—what's the matter with you?

HARPER. You ain't never had no husband!—you *never*, did you?

LUCRETIA. Harper, I did—

HARPER. Liar! . . . You liar! . . . You *never!* You never! Now you just tell me the truth!

LUCRETIA. Oh God!—my arm!

HARPER. (*Exerting more force.*) You been to Roanoke before, haven't you?— Haven't you?

LUCRETIA. I told you—

HARPER. And they run you out, didn't they?—made fun of you and run you out—because you was a . . . a—whore, wasn't you? That's what you was, wasn't you?

LUCRETIA. I wasn't . . . I wasn't, Harper—Harper . . . I . . . I can't . . . breathe!

HARPER. That little old dark man remembered—just upped and remembered!—

LUCRETIA. He's a liar, that's what he is! . . . Sam Green was!—he was! He just—just got killed, that's all! . . . He—was coming back . . . and—

HARPER. Just another lie! Just another . . . lie! That little old dark man . . . He wrote your Momma a letter.

LUCRETIA. (GREMMAR *rises and crosses Down Stage to Stage Right arm chair.*) Momma?

HARPER. Yeah, your Momma! And she wrote him back . . . asking you to . . . to come back home with your sinful self!—your lying, sinful self! You ain't never been no widow! You ain't never been nothing, have you? (*Twisting her arm fully and making her scream, and then letting her go. Simultaneously, as* LUCRETIA *falls,* GREMMAR *sits in chair.*)

LUCRETIA. (*Dropping to the floor and whimpering softly.*) No, no, no, no, no.—no, no!

HARPER. (*Crosses Down Stage Right.*) People laughing . . . calling the preacher a fool! . . . a fool! . . . The preacher!—

LUCRETIA. (*Rising.*) Oh nigger, why—why don't you stop thinking!—stop your . . . your . . . *thinking* and feel something—just . . . just . . . *feel* something!

HARPER. I—I don't deserve no church!—don't deserve none! . . . Making them laugh . . Nothing but a fool! . . . a . . . a fool! Don't . . . don't even deserve . . . God! . . . Not even him! . . . (*Pausing, breathing heavily, thinking.*) He's . . . he's telling me . . . telling me . . . telling me . . . He's . . . Don't even want me! . . . Don't even want me! . . . Don't want me! Don't want me! (*He stands mesmerized—"listening." He turns, stares at her and then starts suddenly toward her. She rises quickly, trying to retreat. He lunges, missing, and then chases her, catching her and ripping her clothing—pawing and mauling and kissing her roughly.*)

LUCRETIA. Harper, don't—don't be crazy! Please don't be crazy! (*He forces her down on the bed. She screams.*)

(*BLACKOUT, except for special on* GREMMAR. *The No. 1 blackout drop is flown in, the No. 3 wall and No. 2 blackout drop are flown out.*)

GREMMAR. (*Softly, distantly.*) He . . . he never did become no minister—Harper . . . Never did . . . Went back to the mines again . . . way down in them mines . . . (*Pause.*) Folks . . . folks told me—told me they never did see much of that man again . . . except that when they did, he was drinking a lot . . . always . . . always . . . drunk. (*Pause.*) He

. . . fell out one day . . . Fell out dead . . . Harper . . . drink on his breath . . .

(*The lights rise slowly in the living room and on the porch, as* GREMMAR *rises and crosses to piano stool and sits. After a moment* HOPE *and* NATE *walk up on the porch, where* LOU *sits staring blankly.*)

NATE. What's the matter, the party over?
LOU. (*Softly.*) No, it's . . . still going on. (NATE *takes* HOPE'S *hand and brings it close to* LOU'S *face.* LOU *looks at the ring, forcing a smile.*) Con—congratulations . . .
HOPE. Hey, don't I get a kiss?
LOU. Sure . . . (*Kissing her cheek.*)
NATE. Getting a sister-in-law, man! (*They go inside,* LOU *again caught up in thinking.*) Hey, everybody, I have an announcement to make! (MILTON *enters from upstairs,* HATTIE *from the kitchen, with* EDNA *following.*) We're engaged!— (*Everyone reacts happily—* GREMMAR *rises and applauds. She grasps her head suddenly and slumps to the floor, groaning. There is a brief moment of stunned silence, and then, near panic as* MILTON, NATE *and* HATTIE *rush toward her, calling her name.* EDNA *begins to cry, while* HOPE *stands with uncertainty.* LOU, *hearing the noise, rushes into the room.*)
HATTIE. (*As* NATE *and* MILTON *hover over* GREMMAR, *trying to revive her, calling her name.*) Louis—quick!—call the doctor! Hurry! Lord, let me get some water! . . . water! (*Rushing toward the kitchen.*)
MILTON. Wake up, Momma!—Momma, wake up!

(MILTON *and* NATE *pick* GREMMAR *up and carry her up to bed, with* EDNA *following—crying.* HOPE *precedes them and turns back the bed covers. As they place* Gremmar *in bed,* Hattie *enters and crosses up stairs with a glass of water. The lights fade to black. In blackout,* Edna *continues crying, as* Gremmar *puts on a bed jacket and the No. 1 blackout drop is flown out. When the change is complete, Edna stops crying, and the lights rise slowly in bedroom.* Lou *stands outside the door to the room.*)

Lou. (*Enters and crosses Stage Center; he pulls chair up to head of bed and sits.*) Gremmar? . . . Gremmar? (*She opens her eyes slowly, weakly, dazedly, seeking him, and looks foggily at him for a moment.*)

Gremmar. Nathan? . . . Is . . . is that you, Nathan?

Lou. (*Softly, hesitantly, somewhat anxiously.*) No . . . it's me . . . Louis . . . Louis. . . .

Gremmar. Louis? . . . Yes . . . yes . . . (*Beginning to fade away.*) Yes . . . yes . . . come up to see me . . . come to see me . . . yes . . .

Lou. (*Quickly.*) How—how do you feel? . . .

Gremmar. (*Still drifting.*) Come up to see me . . . knows I'm not . . . not feeling well . . . yes . . .

Lou. Gremmar . . . (*Pause.*) Gremmar . . . why . . . why didn't you . . . didn't you . . . tell me?

Gremmar. (*Opening her eyes.*) What—what's that, child . . . ?

Lou. Why didn't you . . . tell me? Why— (*Stopping, having difficulty.*) Why did you lie to me?

Gremmar. (*Speaking partly to herself.*) No . . . no . . . no . . . I never . . . I never lied to you, son . . . oh, no . . .

Lou. Gremmar, you did . . . You did . . . (*Smoothing the covers and then watching her sympathetically.*)

Gremmar. Not knowingly . . . no . . . no . . . not knowingly . . . no sir. . . . I wouldn't do that, child, . . . no, no . . . (*Coughing.*)

Lou. Are you . . . all right? (*Pause.*) Gremmar?

GREMMAR. (*Distantly.*) I'm all right . . . (*He takes her hand and begins to stroke it.*)

LOU. You, you always did the right thing . . . always . . . your . . . whole life. So perfect . . . never did anything . . . wrong . . . never . . . lying . . .

GREMMAR. I had my needs, son—yes I did, child . . . oh yes . . . (*Silent again, tired.*) I had my men —yes . . . I was a young woman once, child—yes I was . . . Wasn't always your grandmother, wasn't always tired . . . No, child . . . wasn't always tired . . . (*She reaches for his hand, grasping it.*) No, baby, don't . . . don't close your eyes to my needs. Don't close your eyes. They were real . . . God knows they didn't have nothing to do with right or wrong . . . nothing to do with them . . .

LOU. Gremmar . . . don't . . .

GREMMAR. Don't make me no more than what I was, son . . . Don't fault me for my feelings . . . That's what you're doing . . . that's what you're doing . . .

LOU. Gremmar . . . Gremmar . . . you could have —have said . . . something . . .

GREMMAR. (LOU *rises and steps Stage Left, speaking softly.*) Some things are mine, baby . . . mine . . . just mine . . . I had feelings . . . Yes . . . needed loving . . . touched . . . held— (LOU *rises and steps Stage Left.*) Held in my men's arms . . . That's what my body was for—oh yes! Wasn't easy to be all by yourself in them back woods . . . No, no . . . I had my feelings—

LOU. (*Crosses Stage Center.*) Gremmar . . . just . . . just . . . stop . . . That's just what they think . . . just what they think . . . That we're so dumb . . . Nothing but . . . dumb and . . . stupid and inferior! . . . Sex maniacs . . . degenerate, and all that crap! . . . Lazy . . . black . . . coons! (*Pause.*) You . . . you . . . call them liars and . . . and . . . punch them out and . . . for what? . . . (*Pause, angrier, crossing to bed.*) All this time . . . all this

time . . . you were just the opposite weren't you?
. . . just the opposite . . . just another one of those
. . . those old . . . phonies . . . Just another . . .
phony—

GREMMAR. (*Sitting up.*) I was nothing of the kind!
(*Pause.*) Nothing of the kind! I was a colored woman!
—life in my bones! And they were tender to me! . . .
tender to me! . . . They . . . they understood . . .
They knew! Yes they did! I'm still your grandmother,
Louis—I still am! . . . That's something different,
baby—something different, child—didn't have nothing
to do with you—nothing to do with you and me—

LOU. Gremmar . . . Gremmar, it . . . did! . . .
It did! . . . I—I—who . . . who do you think I
was listening to . . . around here, Gremmar? (*Pause.*)
Doing things. . . . Testifying. . . . Telling those white
kids off! . . . I'm . . . I'm . . . behaving . . . going
to church . . . all that—

GREMMAR. Lord, Louis—Louis, child, get off your
high horse, son . . . Don't be some old . . . old . . .
goody-goody—some old—

LOU. (*Angrily.*) Gremmar, I'm not! (*Hurt.*) I'm not!

GREMMAR. Yes, you are—that's what you are—some
old goody-goody! Talk like some old maid, some—
some little old sissy! Some little old . . . prude—that's
what you are! (*Lou is shocked by her words.*) Lord,
Louis, you're a man, son! You're a man! He gave you
something to use—to use! Don't you know it? (*He
looks at her in disbelief, and with embarrassment.*) It
don't have nothing in this world to do with what you
want to be—don't let folks tell you that!—no it don't!
(LOU *turns away, shaking his head, trying to find a
way to shut out her words.*) Stop thinking there's
something so special about it, Louis—stop thinking so
much and . . . and . . . *feel*, son. That's what you're
missing—that's it . . . It's there, baby . . . Don't
deny it's there—don't deny what it's for.

LOU. (*Turning away.*) I . . . I . . . know what it's

for . . . Don't you think I . . . haven't . . . done
. . . some—some things? Just because I—I haven't
said anything . . . I know . . . what—what it's for!
I . . . don't have to go . . . boasting about it—

GREMMAR. You're ashamed, son—

LOU. Ashamed of——of what?

GREMMAR. Ashamed of us, Louis . . . Ashamed of
your family—your father . . . your mother . . . Nathan . . . and me, too. That's—

LOU. (*Turning to face her—stricken.*) Gremmar, I'm
not ashamed! . . . When—when was I ever—ever—
ashamed? When—when was I . . . ashamed? . . .
I—I have a right to my opinion! Does everybody have
to be—to be the . . . same? What do you mean
ashamed? . . . You—you didn't mean that, did you?
Huh? (*Going to her, grasping her hand.*)

GREMMAR. Yes I did, son—oh yes . . . yes. I seen
you . . . I seen you when I come to your school—I
come there looking for you—I seen you . . . eating
your lunch with your hand in your bag so's nobody
could see what you were eating. I knew what you were
doing! (*He starts to protest.*) You're ashamed—
ashamed of being a black boy! I know it! I can sense
it in you—you're ashamed!

LOU. (*Jerking away from her.*) I was not! I just—
it—it was . . . nobody's business, that's all! I keep
telling you I'm not! . . . I'm not! . . . You're . . .
you're just a . . . a— (HATTIE *hearing the noises,
enters from kitchen and crosses upstairs.*) just a . . .
nigger, that all! That's all you are! Just a . . . a . . .
a . . . sex . . . pot, that's all! . . . Just a nigger!—

GREMMAR. (*Her breathing more difficult.*) Ashamed
of your skin . . . your skin—your family . . . me—

LOU. (Angry.) Just a . . . lying . . . nigger!
You're a nigger, that's what!— (*She begins gasping.
Lou looks at her in horror, yet is caught up in his own
rhythm.*)

GREMMAR. (*Gasping.*) Ashamed! Ashamed! (*He*

moves to her, sitting, grasping her hand, holding it tightly.)

Lou. Will you stop saying that! (*Moving closer to her, his arms around her, rocking her.*) Stop saying that!

Gremmar. Ashamed!

Lou. (*Crying, rocking her.*) A black . . . nigger, that's all!

(Milton *scurries down the hallway, meeting* Hattie. *Together, they rush into the room. Unaware of them,* Lou *huddles close to* Gremmar, *continuing to rock her, and sob.* Hattie *and* Milton *look at him in horror.*)

Hattie. (*With* Milton.) Louis!

Lou. A nigger! . . . Just a nigger! . . . A nigger! . . A nigger!

Milton. (*Lunging, trying to wrestle him away.*) Let—let go of her, boy! You—

Hattie. (*Trying to assist him.*) Be careful now, Milton!— Unhand her, Louis! . . . Louis!

Lou. (*Resisting.*) She knows what she is! (Milton *wrenches him away and begins to half-drag, half-push him across the room.*)

Gremmar. Ashamed!—yes! Ashamed! . . .

Lou. (*Screaming.*) Nigger! . . . Nigger! Nigger, nigger, nigger!— (Milton *drags* Louis *to the stairs and pushes him down them.*)

Milton. Break your neck—break your neck!

Lou. (*Gasping, crying, muttering.*) Just a . . . nigger, that's all—

(Hattie *takes* Gremmar *in her arms and begins to fan and mop the perspiration from her face.* Milton *pushes* Lou *through the living room onto the porch. As they appear,* Nate *approaches.* Milton *shoves* Lou *to the Up Stage Left corner of the porch.* NATE *moves quickly onto the porch to prevent a possible continuing altercation.* MILTON *hovers near* LOU.)

MILTON. You big . . . dummie! . . . Going in there . . . going in there and—and disturbing her and calling her names, and . . . and . . . doing the things you were doing to her! I'll break your neck! (GREMMAR *groans wrackingly. Both* MILTON *and* NATE *turn in horror.* MILTON *moves quickly toward the door.*) Don't you move—don't you move off this porch! You hear me? (*As he goes up the steps.*) Break your neck! (*He hurries upstairs into the room. He and* HATTIE *talk in whispers.* MILTON *takes* HATTIE'S *place, rubbing her arms, while* HATTIE *begins fanning and patting her face. Stunned,* NATE *glares at* LOU, *who rises, turning his back and glancing at him from the corners of his eyes.*)

LOU. (*After a moment, softly, intensely.*) Three of them!—three! . . . Just another—another . . . nigger, that's all! Didn't even marry any of them—not even—not even—one!

NATE. Oh man! . . . You— Lou— You stupid idiot! (LOU *turns and lunges at him, swinging.* NATE *ducks and retaliates, knocking him down.* LOU *rises, charging back. They grapple,* NATE *getting well the better of it.*) You dumb bastard!

LOU. (*Crying, shouting.*) You nigger! . . . black nigger!

(NATE *knocks him down again.* LOU *is ineffective, as* NATE *pummels him.* GREMMAR *begins to suddenly sing, blurting out a song—a spiritual.* HATTIE *and* MILTON *react with surprise and then join her. Oblivious to it at first,* NATE *jerks up, listening.*)

NATE. What the hell . . . They're . . . singing . . . They're . . . they're singing, Lou . . . Lou, listen! (*On his back,* LOU *groans, covering his face.*) Listen

—listen, goddammit! . . . It's . . . her! . . . It's
. . . it's—yeah! I swear to God, it's her singing, man!
(*He moves to* LOU *and pulls him to a sitting position.*)
You hear her, man?—the coarse one? . . . the crackly
one?—the one coming—coming in behind . . . behind
Mom's and Pop's . . . You hear it? (LOU *nods vigorously.*) She—she hasn't done that—I mean, since . . .
since yesterday, you know? I mean—hey—hey—
maybe she's gonna make it, huh? Maybe she's . . .
she's gonna be—be all right. You know, I think she's
gonna do it, man!

LOU. (*Laughing, half-sobbing, half-crying.*) Yeah
. . . yeah . . . yeah! (*The singing stops.* GREMMAR
gasps and is still. HATTIE *and* MILTON *stare at her in
shock. After a moment,* MILTON *nudges her, calling
her name several times. He then sits, dazed.*)

NATE. They've . . . they've stopped singing.

MILTON. (*Slowly rises from the bed, crosses to the
stairs.*) Killing my mother! . . . Killing my mother!—
Killing her!

HATTIE. (*Moving after him.*) Milton—Milton, now
wait a minute!

MILTON. Killing her!—

HATTIE. Milton, will you listen to me! (*As they
move down the steps.*)

MILTON. (*Moving onto the porch and confronting
Lou.*) Killing my mother! Going upstairs, upsetting
her and—and—killing that woman!

HATTIE. (*Moving in front of him.*) Now calm down,
Milton—just calm down. She was— (NATE *gasps
slightly and stands between* MILTON *and* LOU. LOU
stands transfixed, tears welling.)

MILTON. (*His voice breaking.*) Calling her names
. . . calling her names and killing her! (*Lunging toward him.*) I'll kill you, nigger! (*He grabs* LOU. *As
he does* NATE *grasps and struggles with him.*)

NATE. Come on now, Pop—ease up now! He didn't
know what he was saying!—

HATTIE. (*Trying to assist* NATE.) Lord God!—fighting and killing, and she isn't hardly gone! Let go of him, Milton!

MILTON. I'll break his neck!

LOU. (*Gasping crying.*) I'm . . . sorry . . . I'm sorry . . . (*Crying, whispering to himself.*) Oh God! . . . I'm—I'm sorry! . . .

MILTON. No good! . . . No good! . . . You lie! . . . You lie—do nothing but lie! . . . Good as that woman was to you! You ought to be thankful to her as long as you live! You ought to be thankful! I'll make you remember this night . . . *nigger!*

(*He wrenches away from* NATE *and glares at* LOU. LOU *flings himself off the porch, stumbling and falling and crawling a few paces away. Hesitant,* HATTIE *moves quickly off the porch and stands near him.* MILTON *turns and rushes quickly upstairs, where he sits beside the bed, holding* GREMMAR'S *hand. Dazed,* NATE *stands emptily for a moment and then crosses upstairs and sits at the foot of the bed.* HATTIE *sighs heavily, trying to catch her breath, unnerved. She looks toward the house.* LOU *is in a kneeling position on the ground, gasping and crying softly.* HATTIE *turns again to him and sighs, softening somewhat. She moves slowly to him, hovering a moment.*)

HATTIE. Louis, why didn't you do what I told you? . . . I told you to leave it down the drain—that's exactly what I told you!—exactly! (*She turns away, sighing heavily and shaking her head. She looks out into the street, staring blankly, whispering to herself.*) Lord have mercy! . . . (*Taking a step toward him.*) Louis—

LOU. I didn't . . . I didn't . . . mean to . . . to . . . to kill her!

HATTIE. (*Sighing.*) She . . . she was on her way out,

Louis . . . She was . . . We all . . . knew it . . .
we knew it . . . She was going . . . It didn't help
any—what you did, but . . . she was . . . going . . .

Lou. (*Almost uncontrollably.*) I didn't mean to . . .
I was . . . I was just . . . just . . . trying to tell her
how—how I felt . . . That's all . . . I wasn't trying
to . . . to *kill her!*

Hattie. (*Sighing heavily again.*) Well . . . (*Pause.*)
I don't know, Louis . . . I don't know . . . (*Pause.*)
All I know is there's been a lot of trouble around here
tonight.

Lou. (*Stands, crosses to Down Stage Right of
apron.*) I wasn't trying to cause any trouble!— (*Hattie crossing Stage Right to Lou. Lou whispers to himself, trying to control his sobbing but failing.*) I wasn't
trying to kill her!

Hattie. (*Suddenly tired; numb; sounding almost
emotionless.*) That's your father talking, Louis—

Lou. I . . . I . . . loved her . . . I wasn't trying
to hurt her. (*Pause.*) More than . . . than . . . anybody! . . . Anybody! . . . She—she should've known
that! Anybody around here! . . . She knew that . . .
Nate . . . Pop and—and—any of you! She knew that!

Hattie. (*Hurt, trying to mask it.*) I'm . . . I'm
sure she did, Louis, . . . I'm sure . . . (*Turns Lou
around and embraces; he sobs silently.*) It always . . .
always comes so hard when it comes . . . Crashes
down on you no matter what you say you are—like a
fist!—no matter how prepared you think you are for
it . . . (*Sighing again.*) She was a good person, Louis
. . . a good person . . . (Lou *nods slowly.* Hattie
looks toward house and then crosses Stage Left.) Such
. . . such lovely hands . . . lovely . . . Long pretty
fingers . . . You wouldn't have thought it, all the
housework and things she did over her life . . . But
she did . . . (*Looking at her own hands.*) Much as I
try I can't get mine like that . . . Soft, pretty hands
. . . She liked her hands—took pride in them . . .

(*Both are silent, thinking.*) And such . . . a pretty laugh . . . Just as clear as a bell . . . came from way down inside . . . Made her shake all over . . . (*Pause.*) Face would light up . . . eyes would shine . . . (*Both are silent, thinking.*)

LOU. (*After a moment crossing Stage Left to* HATTIE.) She use to . . . to wear that . . . floppy-looking hat out in the sun . . . in the garden . . . (HATTIE *nods.* NATE *rises from bed. He moves to* MILTON, *patting his shoulder, and then crosses down steps through living room to the porch and sits on the bench.*) Made her look like some . . . some creature from out of space . . . some Martian in the garden. . . . (HATTIE *smiles slightly, murmuring agreement.* LOU *pauses, looking out into the street.*) We use to . . . to . . . sit out here at night and . . . see things . . . Make up things . . . Listening to the crickets and things and . . . and staring out into the woods . . . into the dark. (HATTIE *turns, following his glance.*) We'd conjure up things and . . . all sorts of things . . . Cowboys . . . Indians . . . monsters . . . tanks, ships, castles . . . pirates . . . all kinds of . . . crazy things . . . A game . . . just a game . . . (*Pause.*) It's so dark out there now . . . just seems so . . . dark . . . Hardly see anything out there . . . Like—like there was a . . . a . . . power failure and the whole town is blacked out . . . nothing . . . So small . . . so little . . . a big power failure . . . (LOU *and* HATTIE *cross onto porch.* NATE *rises suddenly, reacting to a breeze that has suddenly begun to blow. He opens his shirt, throwing his head back.*)

NATE. Oh man! . . . Oh man, it's about time! . . . It's about time!

(*The lights fade out slowly as* LOU *and* HATTIE *turn toward the direction of the breeze.*)

THE END

PROPERTIES LISTS

Living Room:
    upright piano (Up Right Center) with round stool
    desk Up Right at stairs with straight backed chair
    arm chair (Down Right)
    round dining table (Down Center) with three chairs
    large ottoman (Up Left Center)
    small side table (Up Left of Ottoman)
    arm chair (Down Left)
    floor lamp behind (Down Left) arm chair (not practical)
    small lamp on desk (not practical)
Bedroom:
    wrought iron bed (Stage Right)
    straight backed chair (Up Stage Center)
    small four drawer dresser (chest—Down Stage Left)
Porch:
    bench with two pillows
Act One—Presets—
Bedroom:
    1 pearl necklace in third dresser drawer
    wicker hand fan in third dresser drawer
    5 x 7 photo in third dresser drawer
    folded clothes (3 items) in second dresser drawer
    toy soldier doll (W. W. I) in second dresser drawer
    bottle (small) perfume on top of dresser
    hand mirror with comb and brush set on top of dresser
    hand towel in first dresser drawer
    small dark brown suitcase on bed containing—folded clothes,
        plastic bag of stockings and pair of house shoes
        (Gremmar)
    beige spread on bed with two pillows
Living Room:
    ledger on desk
    pencil and pad in desk drawer
    sheet music (hymns) on piano
Stage Right; Prop Table:
    handball (Louis)
    cup and saucer (Gremmar)
    large brown suitcase (Sam Green)

Stage Left; Prop Table:
  plastic shopping bag (Aunt Edna)
  black patent leather purse (Aunt Edna)
  four glasses iced tea on clear plastic tray (Hattie)
  garden gloves and spade (Milton)
  Scrabble game (Gremmar)
  Bible (Milton)
  cup and saucer with tea (Rev. Mosely)

Act Two; Presets—
  blue table cloth on table
  strike Bible from table
  biology book on porch

Stage Right; Prop Table:
  bid sheets (Milton)
  large gift wrapped package (Aunt Edna)
  wicker clothes basket with clothes (Lucretia)

Stage Left; Prop Table—
  garden gloves and spade (Gremmar)
  Scrabble game (Gremmar)
  small gift wrapped package (Hope)
  pitcher of punch (Nate)
  seven glasses on clear plastic tray (Hope)

On Metal Serving Tray—Louis:
  birthday cake with 16 candles
  paper plates and plastic forks
  cake knife
  one small glass of water (Hattie)
  engagement ring (Hope)

COSTUME PLOT

Act One—
LOUIS:
  levis, faded, straight legs
  brown, blue, white plaid shirt (sleeves up)
  brown belt
  white sweat socks
  brown suede tennis shoes
NATE:
  levis, faded, straight leg, brown belt
  blue button-collar shirt (sleeves up)
  brown sweat socks
  brown suede shoes
EDNA:
  flowered dress
  patent shoes
  patent purse
  beige slip
  beige bra girdle
GREMMAR:
  gray dress with flowers
  black shoes and slippers
  wig
  beige slip
  pearls
HATTIE:
  pink flowered housedress
  brown shoes
  white half slip
  stockings
MILTON:
  beige pants
  work shirt, blue
  brown work shoes
  brown socks

Flash Back—
LUCRETIA:
  beige striped shirt with dark red and cream top

99

    black knee high tie boots
    dark brown opaque stockings
    bra
    slip
    hairpiece (fall)
    petticoat
    pearls
SAM:
    dark brown houndstooth checked pants
    brown and yellow striped shirt collarless
    brown, beige shoes
    brown applejack hat
    brown/black checked vest
    suspenders

LOUIS:
    same as above
NATE:
    tan gabardine pants
    Pressian blue print shirt
    brown shoes with tassles
    brown silk socks
    dance girdle
HATTIE:
    same as top of Act One
MILTON:
    same as top of Act One
GREMMAR:
    same as top of Act One—changes slippers

Flashback—
LUCRETIA:
    dark brown dotted swiss skirt with beige top
    black boots same as first scene
    petticoat—same
    slip—same
    bra—same
    pearls—same
    hairpiece—same
SAM:
    brown checked suit
    brown and white and yellow striped shirt

brown apple jack hat same as first scene
brown and beige shoes

LOUIS:
  same
GREMMAR:
  same

Flashback—
LUCRETIA:
  solid brown dress
  beige apron
  black boots
  brown stockings
  petticoat
  slip and bra
BRITON:
  brown pants
  brown and white striped shirt, no collar
  brown and white shoes
  brown socks
  brown, black and white striped vest
  suspenders

REV. MOSELY:
  grey suit
  navy tie
  light blue and white striped shirt
  cufflinks
  belt
  black shoes
  handkerchief
GREMMAR:
  lilac dressy dress
  beige slip
  pearls
  slippers
HATTIE:
  beige print dress
  brown shoes
  half slip
  stockings

MILTON:
  tan sportcoat
  light brown pants
  beige shirt
  brown socks
  brown shoes
LOUIS:
  navy blue pants
  red, white, black plaid shirt
  black dress shoes
  black or blue socks
  black belt
NATE:
  same as scene before
HOPE:
  blue wrap skirt
  light colored print blouse
  brown shoes
  old necklace
  gold earrings and gold bracelet
  half slip
  stockings

Flashback—
LUCRETIA:
  brown robe
  brown slippers
  slip
BRITON:
  brown pants
  brown and white striped shirt
  suspenders

GREMMAR:
  coral robe and slippers
NATE and LOUIS:
  same as church scene

END OF ACT ONE

Act Two:
NATE:
  levis, same as top of Act One
  brown shoes same as Act One

brown socks same as Act One
brown and beige and blue print shirt
LOUIS:
  levis, same as top of Act One
  brown tennis suede shoes, same as Act One
  white sweat socks
  striped colored shirt
MILTON:
  short sleeved pastel shirt
  brown pants
  brown shoes—same as before
  brown socks—same as before
DRAKE:
  blue shirt
  blue checked pants
  tan hush puppies
  blue socks
  handkerchief
MRS. TOWNES:
  house dress
  shoes
  wig
GREMMAR:
  green print dress
  sun hat
  slippers

Flashback—
LUCRETIA:
  beige print dress
  hat
  purse
  shoes—beige
  gloves
  slip—same as Briton
  wig
  brown hat
HARPER:
  brown striped suit
  vest
  brown plaid shirt
  brown shoes

brown socks
brown belt
brown print tie

GREMMAR:
MILTON:
LOU: } same as top of Act One
NATE:

HATTIE:
  green sleeveless dress
  brown shoes
  slip

MILTON: } same
HATTIE:

LOUIS:
  black pants
  black blue white shirt
  dress black shoes, same as Act One
  black socks

NATE:
  dress pants
  white shirt with print
  brown belt
  brown shoes
  brown silk socks

HOPE:
  two piece ensemble
  slip
  shoes

HATTIE:
  dressy dress
  brown shoes (same ones)

MILTON:
  brown pants (same)
  blue shirt
  brown shoes and socks

GREMMAR:
  same print as top of Act Two

EDNA:
  two piece peach dress
  patent shoes
  slip

Flashback—

LUCRETIA:
  brown crepe satin dress
  hat, same as top of Act Two
  shoes, same as top of Act Two
  bag, same as top of Act Two
HARPER:
  brown suit
  striped shirt
  hat
  shoes and socks
LUCRETIA:
  print dress
  slippers
HARPER:
  change tie
LUCRETIA:
  same as above
HARPER:
  same as above
LUCRETIA:
  housedress
  slippers
HARPER:
  change of shirt

GREMMAR:
  nightgown

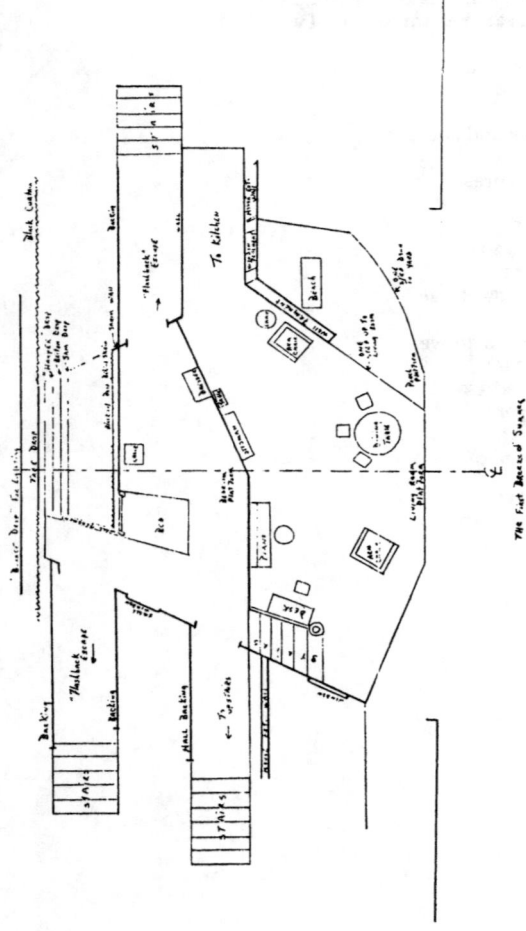

The First Baptist Church Scenery

Also By

Leslie Lee

BETWEEN NOW AND THEN

BLACK EAGLES

COLORED PEOPLE'S TIME

THE RABBIT FOOT

SAMUELFRENCH.COM